Alive and Beating

Alive and Beating

a novel

Rebecca Wolf

ARBITRARY PRESS
New York

For Alisa

"In my life are many windows
and many graves.
Sometimes they exchange roles:
then a window is closed forever,
then by way of a gravestone
I can see very far."

Yehuda Amichai

*M*ONTHS LATER, WHEN THE *dog was gone, too, the tele-vision was left blaring all day for background noise. Silence seemed to magnify the sadness.*

But on that snowy January afternoon before everything changed, our home was abuzz. My three brothers shouted as they ran through the house looking for their shin guards and cleats, ignoring Mom's plea that if they just for once put them in the basket by the front door, they wouldn't be scrambling to find them before every soccer game. Molly barked each time someone ran past her. It was a typical, boisterous scene for our family.

I sat on the bottom step, scratching Molly's belly. The boys kept jostling me as they ran up and down the stairs, although I didn't mind. I would miss them a lot, especially Brian. He was only five. Would he even recognize me when I came back?

"You'd better get used to an all-boy house, Mom," I said. "I won't be back until August."

"Don't remind me!" Mom looked at me tearfully. "I'm glad you have the chance to be in Israel, but I hate that it's six thousand miles away."

"Maybe you'll come visit me?" I felt bad asking, knowing last year's family trip there for Caleb's bar mitzvah had drained our vacation fund, and Grandpa needed a lot of help. Despite my excitement, already I was feeling homesick.

Mom pulled me up from the stairs and hugged me tightly. She twisted my long, black ponytail and kissed me on the forehead. "My head is killing me."

"Do you want to lie down?"

"No, it's okay. Let's get these bags out of the way."

We shoved over the tower of suitcases, and Justin opened the closet door. He grabbed three pairs of cleats from the floor and held them triumphantly above his head.

"Who's a hero now?"

Mom rolled her eyes and groaned. "Go upstairs and tell Caleb and Brian you have the cleats. And then come down and spend a few minutes with Hannah. You're not going to see your sister until the summer." Her voice cracked at the word "summer."

I hoped she wouldn't cry. The internship at the Israel Guide Dog Center extended my semester by two months, but Mom was acting like it was an eternity. I was feeling guilty for being gone for so long.

"You're going to change people's lives," Mom said. "I'm so proud of you."

I couldn't believe my ears. My mother was a pediatrician, and when I told her I was choosing to take care of animals instead of children, she seemed disappointed. This was the first time I felt she approved of my career choice. I beamed with pride.

"Okay, driveway's shoveled, car's cleaned off. Time to go." Dad stomped his boots on the mat as he came in the front door. Molly zoomed over and licked the muddy snow drippings off the wooden floor.

Mom bit her lip. "The flight isn't until six. Why are you taking her so early?"

"The roads are pretty slick, and I don't want to chance getting there late." Dad grunted as he tried to lift one of the duffels. "What'd you pack in here, Hannah? Rocks?"

"Well, I just thought I would have a little more time..." Mom wrung her hands.

"For what? The boys have to be at the Soccer Coliseum soon, anyway."

Mom's eyes welled up and her face crumpled.

"Oh Mom, don't cry." I wrapped my arms around her. We were almost the same height, and we rested our heads on each other's shoulders. "I'll be home before you know it."

"I've never been apart from you for this long," Mom cried. "I'm going to miss you so much."

"I'll FaceTime all the time."

Dad finished loading the bags into the trunk. "Do you want to take Hannah to the airport instead, and I'll deal with the boys? I just thought the bags were too heavy for you, but you could always hire a porter if you need."

"No, one more hour won't make a difference. Saying goodbye is always hard." She called my brothers downstairs, and after I hugged them, she embraced me one more time.

"I love you so much, sweetheart."

"I love you, too, Mom. I'll be back before you know it."

***

*T*HE BUS DRIVER DIDN'T *seem to notice the man in con-struction overalls signaling to stop until he nearly passed him. He swerved and brought the bus to a skidding halt on the roadside gravel just ahead of the Abu Ghosh exit. It was unusually hot for April, and I sat by the window, enjoying the blast of cooled air from the vent above me. I watched the man stumble over the rocks as he ran to the bus. The driver waved in apology as he opened the double doors.*

The man climbed the four steps slowly. He hoisted his body up each, one at a time, grunting with the effort. Without looking at the driver, the man swiped his fare card. He gripped the overhead handlebar as he lumbered down the aisle toward the middle of the bus. He was still panting. Sweat beaded on his brow. His unsteady gait worried me, and I feared he would fall as the driver lurched the bus back onto the highway. The man avoided my gaze, lowering himself into an aisle seat three rows ahead of me, opposite the exit door.

There were about two dozen people on the bus, including a pregnant woman and her bouncy toddler; a teenaged boy with spiked hair and headphones; a middle-aged man reading a newspaper; three off-duty soldiers still in their green army garb; and an elderly couple in the handicapped seats with matching canes hooked onto the metal bar. I sat with my roommate, Keira.

I was happy that Keira and I had decided to dorm together at Hebrew University, even though we hadn't been close friends back at NYU. We came from opposite coasts—I'm from New Jersey and Keira is from California—and we hung out in different crowds. But we lived on the same floor and shared a neighborly intimacy from seeing each other countless times a day. I knew Keira's shower locker was stocked with bottles of shampoo, and I often loaned Keira a phone charger when hers was lost for the millionth time. We both kept our rooms clean and complained to each other that the floor lounge was always such a dump. When we both decided to spend a semester in Israel, it made sense for us to go together.

I yawned and tried to keep my eyes open. There had been a big party on campus the night before to celebrate the start of vacation, and we hadn't finished packing until after two a.m. Keira and I woke early that morning and left our apartment in Jerusalem to catch the 407 bus to the coastal city of Netanya. We planned to stay with Keira's cousin by the beach for the first few days of spring break, before returning to Jerusalem to celebrate Passover.

We were only twenty minutes into the ride, but already Keira was dozing in her seat. She had twisted her body sideways so her knees were pulled to her chest, and her blonde curls bounced up and down with every bump in the road. Even though I was exhausted, I could never sleep in a car or bus. I leaned my head on the window and watched the dirt clouds swelling on the side of the road.

The bus zoomed along the four-lane highway, gathering speed as it neared the steep incline ahead. Just as we passed the Paz gas station at the foot of the hill, I saw the man jump up in the aisle, raise his arms high, and shout. The last thing I heard was a boom.

The bomb hidden under his overalls exploded into a ball of fire, ripping a hole through the side of the bus and spraying nails, screws, and ball-bearings everywhere. Black smoke billowed out from the hole. The roof was charred and bent but still intact. An acrid mix of burning flesh, incinerating steel, and explosives hung in the air. Inside the bus, severed body parts lay strewn on the floor; outside, bloody limbs were scattered as far as fifteen meters away. Eight passengers, including Keira, died instantly, and eighteen others were seriously injured.

The paramedics must have known I was a potential organ donor from the minute they examined me. Unlike Keira, who was a bloody mess and obviously dead, I looked like I was just sleeping, with my head bent down to my chest. My eyes were rolled back, and I was unresponsive to stimuli. The doctors said it was lucky that I barely had a scratch on my body, just the one piece of shrapnel that severed my brain stem.

Kidney One

EARLY SUNDAY MORNING, ON the day her best friend is to marry her ex-fiancé, Leah Weiss wakes suddenly and bolts upright in bed. Her heart races and she sweats beneath her long nightgown. It is unusually warm for early April, and the air in the girls' bedroom is stuffy and stale. For a moment, Leah doesn't remember why she's unsettled. Then reality sets in like a heavy darkness, and her despair is overwhelming.

Leah's head feels too heavy to hold up, and she falls back on the pillow. It's time to give up. She's thought about dying for weeks, even though she wouldn't call herself suicidal. She just can't live like this anymore, with hopes of getting a kidney transplant dwindling every day. And today, unfortunately, she still has to go to dialysis. There's no way out of it.

Leah tiptoes into the bathroom, trying not to wake her three sleeping sisters. She splashes water on her face, and stares at her reflection in the mirror. She looks much older than twenty-one. Her brown hair, once thick and shiny, is now patchy and dull as mouse fur. Even her blue eyes have lost their sparkle. Her cheekbones are sunken, eyes ringed with dark circles. I look like hell, she thinks. No one is going to marry me. Not only am I sick, I'm also ugly. She grips the edge of the sink and squeezes her eyes shut.

"Tamar, this is going to be my last dialysis session." Leah practices looking resolved and calm for when she declares her intentions to her dialysis nurse. "Yes, I know that without dialysis I will die soon. No, my parents do not know, and please don't tell them. No, I do not want to speak to a social worker. Yes, I'm sure." The imaginary conversation drains Leah. She sits down on the toilet and puts her head in her hands.

"Leah? Is that you in there?" Hindy Weiss raps lightly on the bathroom door. "Hello?"

Leah groans. She can never escape her mother. She flushes the toilet and turns on the faucet. "Yes, *Ema*, one minute." She opens the bathroom door and comes face-to-face with Hindy. The sight of her mother's burgeoning belly still shocks her, even though Hindy is nearly seven months pregnant with her ninth child.

"Why are you awake? You need to rest. You have dialysis and then Bassie's wedding tonight." Hindy sighs and rubs her stomach. "I wish I could sleep but this baby is pressing right into my bladder."

Leah tries to slide past her mother in the narrow hallway. With her back facing Hindy, Leah says: "I'm not going to the wedding."

Hindy grabs at Leah's arm and twirls her around. "What are you talking about? Bassie is your best friend!"

"And Moshe was my fiancé! I can't go!" Leah wrestles out of Hindy's grip. Tears well up in her eyes and she bites her lip hard.

"Leahle, don't cry. I know it's hard, but you have to go to the wedding. If you don't, everyone will think you aren't over Moshe and you won't get set up with anyone else."

"I'm not over him! I love him!"

"Oh please! Don't start talking about love. You met the boy for a total of twenty-four hours. You don't even know what love is."

"I know it felt different being with him than with any other boy I've met. Even from the first moment—it's true! He was so kind, really funny, such a good listener." Leah wipes away the tear rolling down her cheek with her sleeve. "And he didn't see me as a pathetic, sick person."

"Leah..." Hindy reaches to stroke Leah's face.

Leah turns away. "He didn't care that I'm sick! His evil parents made him break it off. It wasn't him. I know it."

"Sweetheart," Hindy's voice softens. "It doesn't matter who broke it off. You'll find someone else. Come, let's get you back to bed."

"Do you really think I'm going to find someone else? It was hard enough before. But now that I'm on dialysis—really, tell me." She looks directly at her mother. "Who is going to marry me?"

Hindy hesitates a moment and blinks her eyes. "Leah." She exhales softly. "I pray you will get a new kidney soon..."

Leah's chest tightens. "Don't bother praying, *Ema*. There's no hope for me."

She crawls back into bed and squeezes her eyes shut. The truth is, she can barely remember Moshe's voice, let alone what he looked like. They had gone on their first date last summer, when the sun still hung low in the sky at seven o'clock. Leah had felt like a real woman, dressed in makeup and heels, sipping cappuccino from a fancy porcelain cup in the lobby of the sumptuous David Citadel Hotel. Moshe had been only the third boy she ever dated, but she had decided he was "the one." However, once his mother found out about Leah's worsening kidney disease, he never called her again. And now he was going to marry her best friend. Leah cried into her pillow. So what if her mother is right, and she was in love with love, not with Moshe? Either way, now she's alone.

***

A FEW HOURS LATER, the sun's up and the Weiss household is bustling, except for Leah, who is still in bed. Sundays are the start of the workweek in Israel; the weekend is Friday and Saturday, for the observance of the Jewish Sabbath. Leah's three brothers already left for school. Her three younger sisters eat their breakfast in the kitchen. Rachel, the second-oldest sibling, got married last year and lives in an apartment nearby. Leah's father Yaakov left early in the morning for synagogue and Hindy is getting ready to go to work as a teacher in the neighborhood school.

Hindy peeks into the girls' room and shouts, "Why aren't the beds put away yet?"

"Because Leah is still sleeping," says Rivka, the youngest sister.

"Oy, she's going to be late! Why didn't anyone get her up?" Hindy strides into the room, adjusting her shoulder-length, brown, bobbed wig on her head as she walks. She shakes Leah lightly. "Leahle, let's go. Srulik can't drive you today, you have to take the bus."

Leah buries her head under the blanket. She didn't plan to still be living at home at twenty-one. She thought by now, she would be married with at least one child. That's the way things are in Ramat Eshkol, an ultra-Orthodox Jewish community in Jerusalem with a strict culture that dictates everything from how people dress, to where they work, to whom they marry. Born and bred here, Leah has been indoctrinated into this lifestyle. As the oldest of eight children, she grew up helping her mother Hindy take care of the house and all of her siblings, and to support her father Yaakov in his studies.

Here, the study of the *Torah* and other holy texts is valued above all else. Most of the men do not work. Instead, they dedicate their time to praying and learning. The women do everything else, including working a job (usually teaching), raising their large families, and taking care of their homes. It is a hard life for a woman, but "an honor," as Hindy always reminds Leah, "to support one's husband in the study of *Torah*."

The government pays the men a small stipend for their studies, and a small allowance for dependent children, but money is tight. The Weiss family lives in a spartan apartment typical for the neighborhood, even though most families have at least six children. Their home has three small bedrooms: one for the parents, one for the girls, and one for the boys. The beds in the children's rooms are in a staggered stack like Russian matryoshka dolls, with one pulling out under the other. Every morning the bedding is folded up and stored in a corner to make room for play.

Leah was excited to move out of her parents' cramped apartment and start a life of her own. Like most of her friends, after high school Leah spent a year studying in a religious seminary where she also received a teaching certificate. The matchmaking started for some of the girls right after graduation, and by the end of summer more than half of her class was engaged, even though they were only nineteen years old. That had been the plan for Leah, too. She remembered how excited she was when her mother finally suggested she meet the matchmaker:

"You're going to be a wonderful mother someday," Hindy said, as Leah braided her sister Bracha's hair into pigtails. "You've had so much practice with your siblings, you're a second mother to them."

Leah blushed. Her mother didn't compliment often. "Thank you."

"I think it's time we made an appointment with the match-maker, don't you?"

Leah stopped braiding. Bracha squealed. "Leah's going to be a *kallah*!"

"Hold on, I'm not a bride just yet," said Leah. But she was blushing, excited, and relieved. It had only been two months since graduation, but some of her friends were already engaged. She had been wondering why her mother hadn't called the matchmaker yet, but she was too afraid to ask. "You really think I'm ready?"

"Yes, Leah, I do." Hindy smiled. "You've been ready for a while. It's been me that isn't ready! You're such a help to me. What am I going to do without you?"

But a few weeks later, Leah became sick. She was tired all the time. Her face, hands, and body were swelling, despite her birdlike eating habits. Hindy panicked. "If you don't keep up your figure, we're never going to find you a *shidduch*." She pushed off the appointment with the matchmaker.

Finally, after no amount of dieting would reduce the swelling, Hindy took Leah to a doctor, who diagnosed Leah with glomerulonephritis. At first, Leah's doctor was not that concerned. Glomerulonephritis is a rare disease that sometimes develops after an ordinary strep throat infection when the body gets confused and the immune system produces too many antibodies. These extra antibodies go through the blood and eventually end up in the glomeruli, a part of the kidneys. In most cases, explained the doctor, damage to the kidneys is temporary and the body heals on its own.

Unfortunately for Leah, even when the acute symptoms of the disease cleared up after a few months, her kidneys were irreversibly damaged. The doctor said Leah had developed chronic kidney disease, and at some point in the near future would have to go on dialysis because her kidneys would not be able to filter her blood. Eventually, she would need a kidney transplant.

"Nonsense!" Hindy shouted at the doctor and stomped her foot like a tantruming toddler. "Impossible! A rare disease, a rare complication, and now, a rare treatment! I don't believe it! This is an *ayin hora*, I tell you. That's exactly what's happening."

Hindy firmly believed that someone in the community had put an *ayin hora* (evil eye) on Leah. "Everyone says you are so beautiful and so good you'll get the best boy in all of Jerusalem. Now look at what's happened. People got jealous—and boom! You're sick!"

Leah wasn't sure what to think. She was the valedictorian of her high school, so perhaps a few people were jealous. And it was strange to develop a disease that no one had heard of...but random things occur in the world. Her friend Rachel was born with only three fingers. Her friend Chaya had a brother who was autistic. Her friend Dina lost her father to cancer when she was only five years old. Not everything makes sense.

"You're going to get better, Leahle, I know it." Hindy took a deep breath and forced a smile on her face. She reached over and squeezed Leah's hand. "Just relax. It will all be fine. I am going to visit every rabbi in this country if I have to, but I will get that *ayin hora* removed."

"Mrs. Weiss, with all due respect, no rabbi is going to heal your daughter," said the doctor. "I hope Leah will get better, but I'm being honest when I tell you that I'm afraid she won't. Her kidneys already are only functioning at about fifty percent capacity, and I'm concerned they are going to weaken even further."

"Well, doctor, with all due respect to you, I think you should have a little faith," Hindy squared her shoulders and stood as tall as her five-foot-one frame would allow her. "You believe in science, and I believe in God. Leah will get better. I'm sure of it."

In the hallway outside the doctor's office, Leah started to cry. Her mother gave her a tissue and told her to stop immediately. "You are not going to feel sorry for yourself, and you are not going to make others feel sorry for you. There'll be no more crying—do you understand?" Leah blew her nose, crumpled up the tissue, and nodded yes.

Later that night, Hindy was even more of a drill sergeant than usual:

"Rivka, get those books off the table."

"Leba, take out the plates."

"Bracha, get out the utensils."

"Gedaliah, get the glasses."

"Dovid, Chaim—both of you come right now and set up the extra chairs."

"Yaakov, dinner." Hindy called out to her husband. She ladled out a bowlful of minestrone soup for each girl, a scoop and a half for the boys, and a double portion for her husband. On the table there was a bowl of shredded cheese to add to the soup, and a plate of pita bread piled high.

Yaakov rose from his armchair in the living area and washed his hands with a cup in the small sink on the wall by the table, so he could make the ritual blessing over bread. He gazed at his wife with a quizzical look, but Hindy turned away. "Is everything okay, Hindy? You seem on edge."

"On edge?" Hindy snorted. "Do you know how hard it is to feed nine people three meals a day, every day? It's a miracle I ever seem calm to you."

Leah waited for her mother to tell her siblings that they would have to help out more if Leah didn't feel well and that they should be nice and caring. She thought her mother would set up a system with neighbors for rides or meals or whatever help might be needed, like they do for other families with sick relatives. But Hindy didn't mention anything. Leah sat at the table in silence.

That night before she went to bed, Leah asked Hindy if they were going to discuss her illness with the rest of the family.

"No one can know about this. We don't need people feeling bad for you."

"But it's not like I'm a drug addict or something embarrassing. What's the problem?"

"Do you really want to be part of the Keshet *shidduch* group?"

Keshet was the name of the matchmaking group that matched people with illnesses or special needs together. Leah had heard of it in pitied whispers among the mothers. When there was a Keshet engagement, everyone said, "that's soooo nice" in the most horrific, condescending way.

Leah never allowed herself to consider marrying someone who wasn't perfect. There was so much pressure to be flawless. All of the women in the community seemed to always be put together, and very thin, even after childbirth. Leah wanted to rail against it but a part of her desired those trappings of life. It was easy to just be part of the system, harder to break out of it. And those who did were estranged from their families and had to make totally new lives for themselves.

Leah was too fearful and now, too sick, to do that. She had no choice.

"Okay, *Ema*, I understand."

In their bedroom, Hindy and Yaakov discussed Leah's illness. Hindy instructed Yaakov to learn *Torah* for an extra hour every day so that Leah might merit a recovery from his devout studying. She told him her plan to visit every rabbi she knew to get a blessing for Leah's recovery. She would pray at the graves of great rabbis, of pious women, of Jewish holy figures.

"We'll have trouble with the *shidduch*," said Hindy. "Leah is damaged goods now."

Yaakov grimaced. "She's not damaged! She's wonderful. With God's help she'll be healthy soon and will marry an amazing boy."

"With God's help." Hindy murmured.

Two years later, however, shortly after her twenty-first birthday, Leah was told that her kidneys had deteriorated significantly, and she needed an immediate transplant or dialysis. Leah's siblings were too young to be tested for a kidney match, and neither Hindy nor Yaakov were suitable donors. The doctor said Leah would be put on the national transplant list, and in the meantime, would have to go for dialysis three times a week. He suggested the clinic at nearby Hadassah hospital.

Hindy immediately said no, it couldn't be in a Jerusalem hospital. They couldn't take a chance that someone would see Leah and find out she was sick. Yaakov insisted that they ask their rabbi his opinion about traveling for dialysis, as it would be a burden on Leah, but Hindy refused.

"Srulik can drive her. It will be fine."

Srulik Glassman is a mostly-retired taxi driver whose life was saved almost seventy years ago by Yaakov's grandfather. Both were in France at the start of World War II, and Yaakov's grandfather helped Srulik's parents to hide him with a Christian family. Nearly all of their respective families were killed in the Holocaust, and Srulik and Yaakov's grandfather became de facto brothers after the war, when they both emigrated to Israel.

Since then, any member of the Weiss family who ever needed a ride called Srulik for his free taxi service.

"Srulik is an old man. He can't drive out of Jerusalem anymore."

"Well, he can at least drive Leah to the bus station. We can trust him to keep quiet."

"Hindy, I'm not sure about this. I think she should do dialysis here in Jerusalem."

"No one can know about this, Yaakov. You need to trust me." Hindy rarely stood up to her husband when matters of religion were concerned. "It's so hard for girls these days to find a match, even wonderful, beautiful girls like our Leah. We don't have the money to offer to support a son-in-law. We are already at a disadvantage. You have to trust me."

Hindy couldn't tell the matchmaker the truth about why Leah couldn't be set up with anyone, because if she admitted to a health issue then Leah would be transferred to the undesirables list and be introduced to a boy with either a mental or physical disability. Hindy not only worried about Leah's marriageability, but also that of her younger siblings, because people might worry that disease ran in the family. So instead, Hindy lied to the matchmaker and told her that a relative from America wanted to set up Leah with a cousin of a friend, and he was supposed to be the most wonderful boy in the world, so they would wait for him to visit Israel.

For the past two years, Leah had believed this lie. She saw one friend after another get married, have a baby, start adult life. She was desperate for it, but she believed her mother was right. She couldn't get introduced to someone while she was sick. So, she lived her quiet life, working part-time in the children's clothing store when she felt well enough, rarely going out. But now that she needed dialysis, Leah was despondent. She would never get married. What was the point in hiding her illness anymore? At a certain point, even if she were healthy, she would be too old to be desirable.

Leah kept these feelings to herself. Inside the Weiss house, sad topics were taboo. Hindy's attitude was to be positive about everything and never to worry, because only God was in control. "Remember that God has a plan, even if we don't understand it." She would not indulge Leah in ruminating speculation.

With Yaakov, however, Hindy occasionally let down her guard. Yaakov was more soft-hearted than Hindy, and even though he didn't spend a lot of time at home, he was sentimental.

"Do you remember when she was a baby, how she would pull on her ear while she was drinking her bottle?" Yaakov lay in bed, facing Hindy. "I loved that late-night feeding when you went to bed. Just Leah and me. I never had that with any of the other children."

"Yes, that was sweet. It was our first year of marriage, so you didn't have to go back to yeshiva after dinner."

Yaakov looked into her eyes. "Be honest. Have I been an absent father?"

"What?" Hindy averted his gaze. "What are you talking about?"

"I'm never home, Hindy. I don't spend any special time with the children. And now Leah is going through this crisis, and I haven't even talked to her about it."

"Don't." Hindy pointed a finger into Yaakov's face. "Don't you dare throw her a pity party. She's going to be fine." Hindy turned over and shut her bedside lamp. "I'm going to bed."

***

Back in the beginning of November, when Hindy accompanied Leah to her first dialysis appointment, the rainy season had just begun. It was a particularly chilly day in Jerusalem, and the steady drizzle and gray sky made it feel like winter. The limestone sidewalks were slick from the rain and Leah grabbed her mother's hand to steady herself as they hurried to the Central Bus Station to catch the bus to Tel Aviv.

"What a shame that Srulik couldn't drive us this morning—the weather is so awful," Hindy complained.

"I know I'm sorry, *Ema*."

"And it was very difficult for me to get someone to cover the classroom." Hindy walked so briskly it was hard for Leah to keep up. "And don't forget I will need to be home when the kids break for lunch. And Dovid needs a cavity filled. And your father needs me to resole his shoes. I have so many obligations—God knows how I even do it all. I can't spend hours just sitting with you."

Leah opened her mouth and then quickly shut it. She was quiet for another moment. "I really appreciate you coming with me."

When they got to the bus station, Hindy instructed Leah, "If you see anyone we know, we're going to Bnei Brak to visit relatives. It's close enough to Tel Aviv that people won't suspect anything."

"I wish I didn't need to do the dialysis in Tel Aviv. It will take us at least an hour to get there. Are you sure we can't go to one of the hospitals in Jerusalem?"

"Leah, honestly! I've talked to you about this a million times—why do you still not understand?" Hindy blew the words out of her pursed lips, shouting even as she whispered. "You cannot be seen in the hospital. Not now, not ever. The minute someone sees you are sick, that's it! It's over! You will never find a *shidduch*."

A *shidduch*. That's all Hindy had talked about since the time Leah was nineteen. A match. Someone to marry. Not just someone—the perfect someone. The boy from the wonderful family with the rabbinic lineage and the best Jewish education (and it wouldn't hurt if he had money).

Leah winced. She knew her mother was right. After all, she had been witness to her own cousin Shimon's matchmaking obstacle. Although his clubfoot was fixed while still a young child, he was branded a handicap for life and was only intro-

duced to girls with problems. Leah wanted better for herself. Of
course, she could love someone with a handicap, but she did not
want to deal with one if she didn't have to. "You're right. I just
feel frustrated, that's all."

"I understand, Leah." Hindy patted her shoulder. "I feel
frustrated, too, but I'm sure it's the right thing to do."

Hindy was certain about a lot of things. Her unwavering faith in Judaism, and in particular in her ultra-Orthodox lifestyle, gave her a swift decisiveness. "We have a guide-
book—the *Torah*—so we don't need to worry if something is
right or wrong," Hindy often said. "We follow the *Torah* and
we're on the right path."

Hindy and Leah sat in the very back of the bus, and for
the duration of the ride Leah endured Hindy's complaints:
too noisy, too crowded, too smelly, too long. Leah tried not to
pay much attention. After all, she was going to be taking this
bus three times a week for the foreseeable future. At least she
could do some people-watching in the outside world, which was
a rarity she enjoyed. Leah especially loved to see the different
fashions—the ripped jeans, fringed jackets, leather skirts. All
the women in her neighborhood dressed just like Leah: dark
clothing, very modest, very simple.

The highway signs indicated they were close to Tel Aviv. Leah
felt her heart begin to pound, and her palms started to sweat.
She tried to take a deep breath to calm herself. Out of the corner
of her eye, she peeked at Hindy, but did not say a word to

her mother. A moment later, Hindy grabbed Leah's hand. She squeezed it tight and brought it to her lips for a soft kiss.

"You're going to be okay, Leahle," whispered Hindy. "Don't you worry."

Leah felt a tear drip down her cheek.

"You need to be strong. Don't get so emotional. If you have to, cry in the shower."

She looked at her mother's tight-lipped mouth and tried to muster a smile while blinking away the remaining tears. "I'm okay."

After a second bus ride from the main Tel Aviv bus station to the hospital, they were finally at Ichilov hospital. Hindy and Leah peeked through the open doorway of the dialysis unit. Inside were two rows of six beds apiece, separated by a rust-colored stripe running down the center of the green linoleum floor. Each bed had a wall of monitors, tubes, and outlets behind it; a hemodialyzer machine, rolling tray, and chair by its side; and a small television set hung above. Privacy curtains separated the beds; all were pulled back except for one.

A tall, tanned, young woman with a wide smile and bright blue eyes came to the doorway and waved her hand to beckon them in.

"You must be Leah and Mrs. Weiss," said Tamar Aharoni. "Come in! I'm Tamar, your dialysis nurse. I'm so glad to finally meet you."

Leah blushed, immediately looking down. Tamar exuded confidence from head to toe. Unlike the other nurses in their hospital-issued boxy green scrubs, Tamar wore black, fitted ones with yellow smiley faces printed on her top. She wore her hair in a high ponytail atop her head as if she were ready for a game of beach volleyball. Leah felt drab by comparison in her own gray sweater and long, navy pleated skirt, with her brown hair pulled into a low braid.

Tamar stuck out her hand and Leah looked at it blankly for a second before offering her limp hand for Tamar to squeeze.

"Come, let's find a place for you to sit. There are a few empty beds this morning." Tamar led Leah and Hindy towards a bed in the center of the room. "We have a very nice crowd here. Once you get on a schedule you'll see the same people every time. Don't mind Isaac, though." Tamar pointed to the only bed that was curtained off. "He likes to listen to violin concertos while he rests. He used to be a famous violinist himself, isn't that interesting?"

"Not that bed—go to the one in the corner," Hindy grabbed Leah's arm and hustled her into the bed in the corner of the room. She pulled at the blue curtain next to the chair. "Quick, pull this closed before someone sees us."

Tamar raised her eyebrows at Leah, but Leah just bowed her head. "It's no problem, Mrs. Weiss. I'll close the curtain. Just relax."

"Don't tell me to relax! Do you know what I've been through? What I'm going through?" Hindy's voice was rising along with the color in her face. Leah bent her head even lower and picked at her fingernails.

"I'll be back in one minute." Tamar slid through the small opening in the curtain.

"The nurse seems nice," said Hindy, with a half-smile. She looked at her watch. "But I hope she'll move things along. I really need to get back."

Leah furrowed her brow as she looked at her mother. "I don't know how long this will take, *Ema*. The doctor said it could be a few hours."

"It will be more than that if we don't get things started already," said Hindy. She tapped her foot on the floor impatiently.

Tamar opened the curtain and beckoned to Hindy. "Mrs. Weiss, the care coordinator needs to speak with you. Can you come to the conference room? You'll have complete privacy there."

"But I don't know if Leah needs..." Hindy looked at Leah expectantly.

"*Ema*—it's okay, you can go, I'm okay."

But the moment she was left alone, Leah started to cry. Soundlessly, but with tears streaming down her face.

Tamar returned a few minutes later and saw Leah's tear-stained face. "Oh sweetie, it's going to be okay," she said, crouching down next to Leah's chair and stroking her hair. "I am going to be here with you every step of the way, and I promise you will be okay."

"I'm sorry. I don't even know why I'm crying."

Tamar sat down on the beige spinning stool next to Leah's bed. "I have only one rule for you, and this is it: tell me what I can do to make you happy. None of my patients likes dialysis, but I work hard to make sure everyone is happy anyway."

Leah had never been told to put herself first. "I don't know," she murmured.

"Well, think about it. In the meantime, let's get you going so you can be done and take your mother home. I don't think she's too happy to be here." Tamar winked, and Leah smiled.

"There you go, a smile! I'm successful already." Tamar clapped her hands. "Now, let's get the business talk out of the way, and then we can chit-chat. First—did you get your fistula yet and is it healed enough for us to use?"

Leah rolled up her sleeve to reveal a bulge in her left arm. To allow for easier access of dialysis tubes, and to make Leah's blood flow more easily, a surgeon created a fistula—a combination of artery and vein. Her thick forearm looked out of place on Leah's frail, bony body. "It's so ugly—I hate it," she said. "I guess it's good I always wear long sleeves." She gave a sheepish grin.

Tamar laughed. "I was going to ask you about that later, but yes, if you always wear long sleeves anyway, you're in luck. Okay, and the doctor explained to you about weighing yourself every day to make sure you don't retain too much fluid?"

"Don't worry, my mother makes me weigh myself every day anyway. No one wants a fat bride."

"Wowowow! Another topic to file for later...I've got an over-bearing mother, too. Although her line is that no one wants an old bride."

"You're not married? But you're so pretty." Leah immediately blushed. "I mean...never mind, that was a stupid thing to say."

Tamar squeezed Leah's hand. "That was a sweet thing to say—thank you! No, I'm not married. But we can talk about all that later. Let's finish the important stuff so we can get you started and get you out of here. Okay—food—you know you have to cut down on the sodium and have lots of protein?"

Leah nodded.

"Okay—and what about dialysis? Did the doctor explain to you what's going to happen here?"

Leah nodded again. "He said you are going to clean out my blood because my kidneys can't do it themselves anymore."

"Yes, that's right. Dialysis filters and purifies your blood through this machine here." Tamar pointed to the hemodialyzer next to the bed. "It helps keep your fluids and electrolytes in balance when the kidneys can't, and it removes excess waste and water."

"I understand."

"Great, then let's get started." Tamar unhooked the tubes and inserted two needles into the fistula in Leah's arm. "This might be a bit uncomfortable, but hopefully you won't feel any pain. Just let me know and I'll try to keep you as comfortable as possible."

Leah bit her lip, and a few tears dripped down her cheeks.

"It's normal to be scared. But you'll get used to it. After a while it will hardly bother you."

"I don't want to get used to it," cried Leah. "I don't want to be here!"

"No one wants to be here." Tamar caressed Leah's hair and flipped a few switches on the machine. "Unfortunately, you have no choice right now. You need to do this either until your kidneys heal, or until you get a transplant."

"How long do you think that will take?"

"Well," Tamar hesitated. "I don't know enough of the details of your kidney disease to know whether or not they'll be able to heal on their own. But if you need a transplant, it might take some time."

"How much time?"

"I'm not sure. It depends on whether or not someone in your family is able to donate, or if you have to go on the national transplant list."

"No one in my family will be able to donate," said Leah, in a low voice. "Ow! It's burning!" She squeezed her eyes shut.

"Everything is all set. I can stay here with you for a while and talk, or I can let you rest if you want. It's up to you."

Leah kept her eyes shut. "I think I just want to be alone for a bit please."

"No problem. Your mother won't be back for a while. Should I open the curtain for now?"

"No! I don't want anyone to see me like this."

"Leah, there's nothing to be embarrassed about. Everyone is here for the same reason. And you might find it helpful to talk to people who have been doing this for a while. Like Mrs. Goldstein over there...I think she has a daughter about your age."

"No—please. I just want to be left to myself." Leah tried to twist herself onto her side, but with her arm hooked up she couldn't get into a comfortable position.

"Do you want to watch TV?" Tamar picked up the remote from the wheeled tray next to Leah's bed.

"I don't watch TV," said Leah, flatly. She kept her eyes closed.

"Did you bring a book? Otherwise, we might have some magazines over there by the water machine."

"I'm fine," Leah sighed. "Thank you."

"Okay, I can take the hint. I'll check on you soon."

Leah opened her eyes after she heard the curtain sliding closed. She looked around at her small blue cubicle. This is it, she thought, my new home away from home. She felt an enormous weight on her chest and started to cry again. Eventually she drifted off to sleep.

An hour later, Leah woke up to see her mother sitting next to her. "*Ema*? How long have you been here?"

"Just a little while," said Hindy. "Poor *mamale*, all these tubes and wires and needles. It looks awful."

"It's not so bad," said Leah, as she tried to sit up straight in the bed.

"I hope it's done soon. I really need to get back." Hindy pressed the call button on the bed. "Where's that nurse?"

Tamar appeared a moment later and quickly pulled the curtain closed behind her. "Are you okay, Leah?"

"She's fine," said Hindy. "But this is taking a very long time. Can we make it go any faster? We really need to get back, and the bus takes forever."

"Where are you coming from? Bnei Brak?" Tamar asked.

"No, no. Not from there. No need to ask so many questions," Hindy snapped. "Please tell me—can you make this go any faster?"

Tamar checked the readings on the monitor. "I'm sorry Mrs. Weiss, but I can't. I would estimate Leah has about two more hours to go. We can call her a cab if you need to leave."

"No, I'll wait—I took today off from work anyway, but I need to get back for the children."

"You work outside of the home, Mrs. Weiss?"

"Of course I do!" Hindy puffed out her chest proudly. "I'm a third-grade teacher. How else would we have any money? The *kollel* barely pays anything, not that I'm complaining." She looked at Tamar. "You know that a *kollel* is a holy place where the men learn *Torah* all day and into the night?"

Tamar nodded. "Yes, of course! I'm Jewish, you know. I even learned *Torah* in school."

"Well," Hindy waved her hand towards Tamar's nose ring. "Your business is your business."

Leah groaned and pulled at her mother's hand. "*Ema*! Stop!"

"Like I was saying, our men do not work regular jobs. They study all day and women do everything else, including working, taking care of the children, cooking, cleaning...everything! It's hard, but it's an honor to support one's husband in the study of *Torah*."

"That sounds very hard. I admire you."

"Thank you," said Hindy, smiling.

"And you look like you are expecting another child?"

Hindy patted her stomach. "Yes, *Baruch Hashem*. In a few months."

"How many children do you have?"

"So many questions!" Hindy clucked her tongue. "We have a big family, *k'nina hora*. No need to count our blessings."

Tamar knelt down by Leah's head. "Are you feeling okay? Any headaches?"

"Yes...a bit." Leah started to cry again.

"Leahle! Don't cry!" Hindy wiped Leah's cheeks with the back of her hand. "It's almost done and you're fine. Stop crying."

Tamar whispered to Leah, "Should I tell your mom to go?"

Leah shook her head no, and she adjusted herself in the bed again. "Just something for the headache, please."

At the end of the session, Tamar gave Leah another hug. "It was so nice to meet you. I can't wait to see you again in a few days."

***

A FTER SEVERAL WEEKS OF dialysis, the long bus rides from Jerusalem were taking a toll on Leah. She trudged into her dialysis appointment looking ragged and frail.

"Were you out partying again last night?" asked Tamar.

"Not really," said Leah, managing a small smile. "It's the travel. I have to get up at six to get the bus to the Central Bus Station and then another bus to get to Tel Aviv and then another bus to get to the hospital by nine."

"Poor girl. I wish someone could drive you."

"My mother can't drive me," said Leah defensively. "She works, you know, and we only have one car."

"Wait, I have an idea!" Tamar rushed out of the room. A few minutes later she returned, looking very excited. "Okay," she said. "It's all set!"

Leah looked quizzically at her.

"Please hear me out before you say no," said Tamar. "I just spoke to my brother Benny. He's a compliance officer for Teva Pharmaceuticals. He works near here in Herzliya, but at least twice a week he needs to visit the plant in Jerusalem. He leaves around the time you're done with dialysis and he can drive you home today. He'll be waiting outside at noon."

"I can't," Leah said. "Ride home alone in a car with a strange man? No. That wouldn't be proper."

"But you're exhausted," Tamar said. "Dialysis drains your energy. Wouldn't it be a relief to just sit back and relax instead of hurrying around trying to catch a hundred different buses? Besides, Benny isn't a strange man. He's my baby brother! Trust me, with three older sisters, he's been trained to be the perfect gentleman. Oh, and he's gay. So, you don't have to worry about him putting any moves on you." She smiled reassuringly.

Leah felt the heaviness of her exhaustion in all of her limbs. She didn't know if she even had the energy to walk through the bus station. "Well...maybe just for today. But there are rules for being alone with a man. I'll have to sit in the backseat, and the doors will have to be unlocked. I think a window might also have to be open." Although as she ran through the list of rules in her head, she wondered if they even applied to a gay man. A gay man! She had never met one before. No one was gay in Ramat Eshkol.

"I'm sure Benny won't mind. He'll love the company. I think you will, too."

A few hours later, Leah met Benny outside the main lobby of the hospital. He was waiting in front of his white Mazda 3 sedan. When he saw her, he opened the back door and swooped down low in a bow. "You must be Leah. It's my pleasure to serve you."

"Oh my gosh, thank you so much Mr. Aharoni," stammered Leah, blushing. She was entranced by his smooth, shaven head, the black-framed glasses perched on his forehead, his taut muscles straining the buttons on his shirt. What a contrast to the heavily bearded, black-hatted, black-suited men who lived in Ramat Eshkol. He certainly didn't look the way she imagined a gay man would.

"Call me Benny. And I'll call you Miss Leah, like from *Driving Miss Daisy*," said Benny, chuckling.

"What?" Leah felt flustered.

"You know, the movie with the old lady and the chauffeur?" Benny turned around from the front seat, smiling at Leah.

"No, I'm so sorry. I don't really watch movies." Leah felt embarrassed that their first exchange was going terribly. She worried that he would think she's dumb. Or some kind of weirdo.

"Never mind, I hated the movie anyway. Okay, *yalla!* Let's go!"

Benny and Leah chatted the whole ride to Jerusalem. He told her about the attempted break-in of his car, and how it was the third time someone had tried to steal it off the street.

"That's terrible! You must be so upset."

"It happens." Benny rested his arm on the open window and held the steering wheel with the other hand. "Robbery is a fact of life. Nothing to get worked up about."

"It's not a fact of life in Ramat Eshkol. We don't even lock our doors."

"You're joking."

"Not at all." Leah sat up straighter in the backseat. "We look out for each other. It's like one big family. One neighbor watches another's baby so she can do the food shopping for both of them. We lend our best jewelry to the bride and her mother. Everyone cooks for the person who is sick. You know, things like that."

"No, I didn't know," admitted Benny. "That sounds very nice. I don't even know half of the people in my apartment building."

"You should come visit sometime," said Leah. As the words escaped her mouth, she regretted them. Who was she kidding? Benny would stick out like a sore thumb. He would judge them for being provincial and they would snub him for not being religious. And if they found out he was gay, who knows what would happen? She slouched back down.

"I would love to. I'm sure it's very different from Tel Aviv. It's definitely much cooler. I can't believe only an hour's driving distance can make such a difference in the weather."

Leah was relieved to discuss more mundane topics. She told Benny about the time last winter when it snowed two inches and all transportation within Jerusalem was paralyzed. He laughed at her description of trying to take her younger siblings sledding in the paltry snow.

"Okay, here we are!" Benny pulled up in front of the Central Bus Station in Jerusalem. "Are you sure I can't drive you straight home?"

Leah couldn't believe they were already in Jerusalem. The ride had gone so quickly. She was surprised by how much she enjoyed talking to Benny. It was the first time she ever had a conversation with a man outside of her community. Not that she ever really had a conversation with an unrelated man in her community. Even her father only gave her a few minutes of attention each day. With ten people in the family, there was barely room at the table to fit all of them for dinner. Anyhow, her father and brothers generally sat at one end of the table and her mother and sisters at the other.

"No, no, this is perfect. Thank you so much. I can't tell you how much I appreciate this."

"It's no problem. I enjoyed talking to you." Benny smiled at Leah. "I'll see you again on Wednesday."

"Oh, no, that's okay. I told Tamar just this once."

"Don't be ridiculous—you're doing me a favor. I'm so bored driving that long way by myself. See you Wednesday."

Before she could protest any further, Benny drove off. Leah smiled the rest of the way home.

A few days later, Benny again waited by the lobby to drive Leah home. "Miss Leah! So good to see you again!"

"Hi Benny," said Leah, blushing. She thought he was even better looking than the other day. "It's nice to see you, too. Thank you so much for driving me."

"How's the temperature back there? Do you want me to make it warmer?" He caught Leah's eye through the rearview mirror.

"It's fine. Whatever you want."

"What do you mean, whatever I want? I asked, what do YOU want?"

"I have no preference."

"No preference!" Benny laughed. "Ha! That's a good one. Women always have preferences. I have three sisters. I know."

"I really have no preference."

"About anything?"

"Well, of course, about some things, just not this."

"Okay, chocolate or vanilla?"

"What?" Leah was starting to squirm.

"Chocolate or vanilla?"

"They're both good."

"Leah!" Benny stopped at a light and turned around to look at her. "You *do* care. I know you do. I'm sorry you've been raised to think you can't have an opinion about anything, but you can, and you should! We're stopping for ice cream right now and you are going to pick a flavor!"

"You're crazy!"

"I happen to be very hungry, so this argument came at the perfect time," said Benny, turning onto a side street and pulling up in front of an ice cream parlor. "Now let's go inside and you order for yourself. My treat, no discussion."

He forced Leah to order first.

"Wait, I need to make sure it's kosher." Leah looked at the wall next to the cash register and saw the kosher certificate hanging on a frame. "Okay, a small cup of pistachio, please."

"Pistachio? I'm shocked!"

As the weeks went by, the misery of dialysis was tempered by Leah's enjoyment of her time with Benny. Talking to him felt revelatory to her, as if Benny was peeling away layers and helping her imagine possibilities. She confided in him about why she had to do the dialysis in Tel Aviv, explaining that her illness had to be hidden or she would never get married.

"I don't understand," Benny said. "If you are all so nice to each other and help each other out all the time, why is there such a stigma to being sick? Why are you worried that no one will marry you?"

Leah bit her lip. She had thought about this a lot ever since Moshe broke off the engagement. At first, she was angry—incredulous, even. But as she felt herself become a weakened shell of who she used to be, she accepted and understood it.

"You don't understand because you are not in my world. You think the women in our community are weak because we serve our husbands. But you see us all wrong. Women are strong. We work, we raise families, we cook, we clean—we do everything so that the men can focus on their *Torah* studies. A sick woman can't do that for her husband."

Benny made a whirling motion with his hand. "Keep going."

"If I would marry someone that would be okay with my limitations, that means he would be less of a person himself. He would be willing to share some of the household duties, and he might be okay with not having as many children. That's not who I want.

"That's not who you want, or that's not what your parents want?"

Leah stopped to consider this. She had always been told that she was so special, she should get the best scholar in all of Jerusalem. Well, only her mother said this to her.

"I'm not sure. But I just don't think I'll ever get married."

"Never get married? Are you crazy!" Benny slammed his hand on the steering wheel. "Miss Leah, some of the things you say are really ridiculous."

"No, it's true. My cousin Shimon had a clubfoot that was fixed by the time he was three years old—you couldn't see anything wrong! But people in the community knew about it, and in the end he was married to a girl with a limp."

"So what? A limp? Who cares?" For the first time in all their conversations, Benny sounded angry. "I have eczema. Tamar has two toes fused together. So what? No one is perfect!"

"I'm sorry, I didn't mean to upset you."

"Upset me? Stop thinking about how other people feel. Start thinking about yourself." Benny pulled over to the shoulder of the highway so he could turn around and look at Leah. "Do you know how hard it was for me to come out to my parents? My father is your typical tough Middle-Eastern man. He fought in forty-eight, in sixty-seven, in seventy-three. Took bullets in all of them and I don't think he cried once. I'm just the opposite, but I always pretended I was like him. Finally, one day I just realized that life is short, and I don't want to live a lie all my life."

Leah looked down at her hands. Benny reached and lifted her chin up. Her cheeks burned, and she jolted from his touch. No man other than her father had ever touched her face.

"You need to listen to me. You need to live an authentic life. So what if the matchmaker doesn't want you? Pop into a bar for ten minutes and I guarantee you'll have three guys vying for your attention."

Leah looked blankly at Benny. He stared back for a moment, then turned the car around and pulled back onto the highway.

"If the worst happens," he said, "and you don't find a husband, go make something of your life, anyway. Don't just wait around. Old cheese gets stinky."

Leah thought about that conversation a lot over the next few months. She was still obedient and did everything to please her mother, but she wondered about her future. What if she didn't get married? Should she still work in the back room of a children's clothing store? Why shouldn't she go to college and get a real job? Maybe become a nurse like Tamar? She felt tethered by her dialysis, though, and any real dreams seemed to be just that—dreams. Leah couldn't imagine really moving on with anything in life when she had a three-times-a-week dialysis commitment that consumed both her time and her energy. More than that, she couldn't imagine a life outside of Ramat Eshkol. It's where she'd grown up and where she belonged, even if she didn't fit in anymore.

***

O N THIS SUNDAY MORNING in April, it seems to Leah like it's the millionth time she's come for dialysis. She pulls the blue privacy curtain closed and flops into her usual chair in the corner, tucking her skirt around her ankles. The pungent antiseptic fumes burn her nostrils. She's exhausted, but she can't sleep until the needles are in. Beneath the curtain, she spies Tamar's neon orange sneakers and feels the knot in her chest loosen just a bit.

"*Boker Tov,* sweetie! Don't you look pretty today!" Tamar slides in through the crack between the curtain and the wall. Her blonde hair is in a high ponytail atop her head, and it swings as Tamar pulls over a swivel chair to the hemodialyzer.

"I look how I always do." Indeed, Leah is dressed in her usual way: a navy, long-sleeved, buttoned shirt, tucked into a gray, pleated skirt that flows past her slim hips and reaches her ankles. Her legs are covered in opaque nude stockings, and she wears black slip-ons with rubber soles. "I like your scrubs today, Tamar. Are they new?"

Tamar is wearing a pink top printed with fuchsia hibiscus flowers, with matching pink pants. She never wears the hospital-issued green scrubs. "Yes! Thank you for noticing, sweetie! They're perfect for the start of spring, don't you agree? I love April. Everything is budding. It's a time of possibilities." She finishes adjusting the hemodialyzer and snaps on her latex gloves. "Ready, one, two, three..."

"Ow," whispers Leah. She bows her head and pulls at her thin brown braid while Tamar injects the lidocaine into the thickened part of her forearm. "Ow...it burns so much." A tear rolls down Leah's pale face. "After all this time, even the numbing medication still hurts so much. I'm such a wimp."

Tamar wipes the tear off Leah's cheek with her gloved hand. "You're not a wimp. This is hard, but it's better than being dead."

Leah turns her head away, trying to sit up straighter, while her left arm remains on the armrest, tubes attached. The hemodialyzer whirs to life, and Tamar gets up from the stool. "I'm sorry we barely got to chat, but Shira is out today, and I have to cover her patients."

Leah bends her head down to her chest. Tamar squeezes her hand.

"Are you sure you don't want to watch TV? And you definitely want the curtain closed? You're not bored? You could talk to the other patients—you have more in common than you think."

Leah shakes her head and picks up her book of Psalms. She begins mumbling her prayers quietly. Tamar stays for a moment, biting her lip. Then she blows Leah a kiss and walks away.

Through the sliver of an opening in the curtain, Leah peeks at the chair next to hers. A familiar middle-aged woman is talking animatedly to someone next to her. Leah can't see him, but it's probably Isaac, the old man who blares classical violin music too loudly. She shifts in her chair and stares at the curtain. Tamar is right, dialysis is boring. But Israel is a small country; one person is connected to the next with only a few degrees of separation. Leah can't risk talking to anyone. She hears her mother's voice in her head: "If people know you are sick, you will never get married."

Leah sighs and tries to focus on her prayers, but the words blur on the page. She needs to tell Tamar that this will be her last dialysis session. She is tired of the treatment, the travel, the deceit. She'll continue to leave her house at the appointed time three days a week, so her parents won't suspect anything. It's better than confronting them.

Leah twists her ponytail and crosses and uncrosses her legs. She knows this isn't a perfect plan. Until she can tell her parents, she'll be living a lie. Praying for a brilliant idea, she closes her eyes, and dozes off.

About an hour later, Tamar comes in to adjust the blood pressure cuff on Leah's arm, trying not to wake her.

"Oh, I'm sorry!" Leah sits up and rubs her eyes.

"What are you sorry about? I'm the one who's sorry. I was trying not to wake you, but the cuff came loose, and I wasn't getting the right reading."

"It's fine." Leah smooths her skirt so that it covers her legs completely. "I didn't mean to fall asleep."

"It's a good thing Benny is driving you home today. I don't think you're in any shape to take the bus later. You look absolutely exhausted." Tamar tilts her head sympathetically.

"I am tired," Leah admits. "Lately, I've been so wiped out. It's hard on my mother because I'm just a wet rag when I get home. I can't help with anything, And she has so much cooking and cleaning to do, especially with *Pesach* coming in just a few days."

Tamar bends down by the hemodialyzer machine, surreptitiously rolling her eyes.

Leah squirms in her seat. "Tamar, are you sure it isn't a bother for Benny to drive me? He's always so nice about it, picking me up at the hospital and everything. I feel terrible that I can't return the favor."

"Return the favor? You have no idea how much Benny enjoys talking to you. He says the commute feels so much quicker with you. You have a great sense of humor, and you make him laugh the whole way."

"Me?" Leah blushes. "I'm not funny at all."

Tamar laughs. "See, there you go again, so deadpan. I love it!"

She inputs her data into Leah's chart, then smooths Leah's hair. "You still have two more hours to go, sweetie. Why don't you rest some more, and I'll wake you when you're done?"

Leah smiles gratefully at Tamar and closes her eyes.

***

A FEW HOURS LATER, Tamar comes back in and turns off the hemodialyzer machine. "All done! That went by pretty quickly, didn't it?" Leah gives her a half-smile, but her eyes are dull. A bell dings from the other side of the room. "One sec, I need to check on Mrs. Goldstein. I'll be right back to unhook you from all this stuff."

Just as Tamar steps away, Leah's phone rings. She flips it open (smartphones with Internet are not allowed in her community) and hears Benny's voice on the other end.

"Leah, hi it's me, Benny."

"Benny!" Leah blushes. He rarely calls her, usually only to say he's running late. "Are you going to be late again?"

"Well, that's a nice way to say hello. I'm fine. How are you?" Leah hears the chuckle in his voice, and it elicits a smile from her for the first time today. "I'm calling to tell you that unfortunately, I won't be able to drive you back to Jerusalem today. I'm afraid you'll have to take the bus."

"Ohhhhh." Leah can't hide the disappointment in her voice. "That's too bad. Why not?"

"There was a bus bombing on Route One—terrible, so many dead—and now the road is closed in both directions. I'm sorry, but I'll never get to Jerusalem in time, so I'm going to visit the plant tomorrow instead." Benny says. "Sorry, Miss Leah! Will see you soon!"

Leah sits there, holding the phone in her hand, feeling its useless weight. It must be a sign from God. No one is meant to stop her.

Benny might have been able to, Leah thinks, even though they are from different worlds. She found herself telling him things she had never even told Bassie, like how she had watched some movies at a friend's nonreligious relatives' house, or how she wished she could go to Disney World. Surely Benny would have forced Tamar to tell her parents, or maybe he would even have told them himself. He would have seen that Leah doesn't really want to die; she's just trapped. She begins to cry.

Tamar comes over to unhook her from the tubes and needles. "I just spoke to Benny. He told me he can't drive you today. I'm sorry. I can't believe there was a suicide bombing. I thought those days were behind us. It's so awful! All those people...I can't even bear to watch the news." She wipes away a tear.

Leah, too, tries to compose herself, dabbing her nose with the edge of her sleeve. She can't talk to Tamar now. "I have to go. Thank you." She fumbles for her bag, pushes away the blue privacy curtain, and quickly heads for the door. She can feel Tamar's eyes on her back, but she doesn't look around.

Leah trudges out of the hospital, the courage and energy seeping out of her with each step. The cacophony of traffic noise makes her wince. Her phone rings—it's her mother.

"*Ema?*"

"Chaim has a fever and a sore throat, so I need to take him to the doctor. I'll meet you at the wedding. Don't be late!" Hindy hangs up before Leah can say anything.

"I'm fine, *Ema*, thanks for asking." She stifles a sob, but tears stream down her face. Tears stream silently down her face. Her feet are two concrete blocks. She plods slowly down the street, not caring how strange she may look to others.

Maybe my bus will be bombed, she thinks, and then it will all be over quickly. Would that hurt? But Leah then realizes her usual bus won't be running. None of the buses on Route One will; she'll have to take the 443 one along Modiin Road. Her stomach hurts in anticipation of the roundabout, winding highway that always nauseates her and takes twice as long.

Leah despairs, thinking about how she'll be late for dinner. And Bassie's wedding! She smacks her forehead. Her mother will be furious. But at least now, Leah thinks, she can get out of going. Of course, her mother's retelling of the wedding might even be worse than going! She'll have to hear about how beautiful Bassie looked, and about all of her other friends and their husbands, and those few poor, pathetic girls who are still single...

Suddenly Leah can't take another step. She sits down on a street bench, takes out her phone and dials Benny, but the call goes straight to voicemail. What an idiot I am, she thinks. What am I even doing calling him? How can someone like him save me? She shuts off her phone and stuffs it in the bottom of her bag.

***

IN JERUSALEM LATER THAT evening, Hindy steps out of the crowded wedding hall and tries Leah's phone for the hundredth time. Still no answer. Hindy goes back into the thunderous noise and stands by the wooden partition that separates the men and women. On the other side are a dancing mass of black-hatted, black-jacketed, bearded men. "Tzvi," she calls to one of the boys. "Can you please go get Reb Yaakov Weiss? Tell him his wife needs him."

A few minutes later, Yaakov meets Hindy in the hallway. He wipes the sweat from his brow with his handkerchief. "What a wedding! Did you see Bassie's father high up on the chair?"

"Yaakov, I'm really getting worried," Hindy interrupts her husband. "Leah is missing Bassie's whole wedding!"

"She didn't want to come. And I understand. It's hard for her."

"You don't understand any of it," snaps Hindy.

"Maybe if you would talk to me about some of these things instead of leaving me in the dark, I would be able to understand more."

Hindy opens her mouth, but Yaakov waves his hand across her face. "You are too tough. I know you have to, to manage everything, but sometimes...I don't know...sometimes you are just too tough."

Hindy's phone rings. "This better be Leah."

"Hello, Mrs. Weiss, this is Dr. Levine calling. I have great news! We have a kidney for Leah! I tried calling her, but I kept getting her voicemail."

"A kidney? How? She's only been on the transplant list for six months. I thought you said this would be a very long road?" Hindy stands completely still, as if in a trance.

"Put it on speaker! I need to hear this!" shouts Yaakov.

"There was a sudden death of a person almost exactly the same age and size as Leah, and of course the same blood type," explains Dr. Levine. "It should be a good match. And the donor kidney is in Jerusalem, which is crucial, because time is of the essence. The kidney needs to be transplanted within twelve hours."

"Twelve hours?" Hindy stammered. "I...I...I can't believe it."

"I need you at Hadassah University Hospital-Ein Kerem within four hours so we can start prepping Leah."

"Hadassah? No. No. No!" Hindy shouts, adamant. "Not in Jerusalem. And what if the donor is not Jewish—then it might be a problem. We need to call the rabbi; it will take time."

Yaakov takes the phone away from Hindy and yells into the speaker: "We'll be there."

"Are you crazy?" Yaakov wheels around and grabs Hindy by the shoulders. He is right up against her, his words spewing out and droplets of saliva hitting her in the face.

"What are you doing?" Hindy tries to push his hands away. "People are watching!"

"What are YOU doing!" Yaakov roars, shaking her shoulders. "I've sat by for too long watching you torture our poor Leah, making her shlep to Tel Aviv, hiding her in a closet. No more! This is her chance, and we are not going to give it up." He steps back and paces the hallway.

"I'm not asking any rabbi. This is God speaking to us loud and clear. A young person, Leah's age, just died. Parents just like us are preparing to bury their child and you are going to turn away the gift of life? It's like the story of the drowning person who asks God why He let him drown, and God says: 'I sent a rowboat in the middle of the ocean, what other miracle were you waiting for?'"

Hindy stands frozen, mouth agape.

"I have faith that God will take care of our Leah. This is our miracle. I'm going to look for Leah. Are you coming?"

Lungs

SHORTLY AFTER YAEL GLASSMAN puts her daughter, Tikva, to sleep on Saturday night, she steps on the scale:
forty-three kilos. She groans, nudging the scale back under the
bathroom sink with her foot. The doctor said she needs to weigh
forty-five kilos, or one hundred pounds, before she can safely
move out of her parents' house. Right now, she's too frail and
weak. Yael tries to sigh, but can't take a deep breath, and starts
to cough. It's an unusually warm night in April, but Yael is still
cold. Who am I kidding, she thinks. I'm getting worse every day.
I'm running out of time.

"*Ema*, is it good?" Tikva calls from their bedroom.

"Yes, *booba*, my sweetie, it's good." Yael lies.

"Hooray for you, *Ema*!" Tikva claps her hands loudly. "I
knew you could do it."

Yael feels a pit in her stomach. She can deal with her parents, but disappointing her eight-year-old daughter is the worst.
Tikva has been asking to move back to their apartment for two
months, ever since Yael got out of a lengthy hospital stay for
her latest bout of pneumonia. The fun of a sleepover at her

grandparents' place has worn off for Tikva. Yael understands the need for personal space. She feels it intently for herself.

"Go to sleep now, Tiki. You have to wake up early for school."

"Don't be noisy when you come in!"

"I won't. Now go to sleep."

Yael and Tikva have been sharing the small bedroom in the same four-room apartment in which Yael was raised, in Beit Hakerem, a mostly secular neighborhood in southwest Jerusalem. Her parents, Srulik and Manya Glassman, sleep in the other bedroom, and they all share the tiny, white-tiled bathroom in the middle of the narrow hallway. There is a small kitchen that opens into the living room, and a wide concrete balcony that overlooks one of the many parks for which Beit Hakerem gets its nickname as one of the few "green neighborhoods" of Jerusalem.

Manya gets up from her chair when Yael walks into the kitchen and looks with eyes wide with concern. Wordlessly, Yael shakes her head no. Manya grimaces, her thin lips disappearing into her mouth, then goes to the refrigerator and takes out the eggs and butter. She cracks two eggs into the glass bowl on the counter and uses her finger to wipe the remaining membrane from inside the shell into the bowl.

"*Ema*, that's disgusting. Why do you do that?"

"We never waste food." Manya sighs. "Do you know what my mother would have done for a little bit of egg during the war?"

Of course, Yael knows. She has grown up in the shadow of the Holocaust, as either a first- or second-generation survivor, depending on which parent. Manya was born shortly after the war in a displaced persons camp, to parents who had miraculously survived concentration camps in Poland. Srulik had been a hidden child in the Holocaust, cared for by a Christian family on a farm in northern France, while the rest of his family in Paris were killed by the Nazis. Although Yael doubts Manya can remember much about her early childhood, rarely a day goes by when Manya doesn't mention the war in some way.

"Have you been eating properly?" Manya whisks the eggs while the butter sizzles in the frying pan.

"Yes. You were with me all day today, *Ema*—you saw me eat."

"Are you taking your enzymes?"

"Yes!" Yael hears her voice rising and quickly shuts her mouth. She doesn't want to yell at her mother, and she especially doesn't want Tikva to get out of bed. "This recovery has been especially hard," she whispers. "The infection is much better but it's still hard to breathe, and I'm always tired. I guess I'm using so much energy just to function that I'm not able to gain weight."

Yael has cystic fibrosis (CF), a genetic disease that causes the body to produce abnormally thick, sticky mucus. The mucus clogs the lungs, causing persistent and often-life threatening lung infections, and obstructs the pancreas, inhibiting the ability of the intestines to break down food and absorb vital nutrients. She was diagnosed before her first birthday, when her mother confided in the pediatrician that she didn't like kissing baby Yael because her skin was too salty. It was a tell-tale sign of CF, and helped to explain why Yael wasn't a chubby baby, despite the endless feeding, and why her breathing was so loud.

"Maybe it's time for the NG tube again," murmurs Manya. She deftly flicks the pan and flips the eggs to the other side.

"No!" This time, Yael doesn't try to quiet her voice. She hates the naso-gastric feeding tube that goes up through her nose and into her stomach. She used it for years in her early twenties when her disease worsened and her weight plummeted; she could never get used to the relentless discomfort.

"Well, what do you suggest then?"

"I don't know." Yael puts her head in her hands. "I can't believe I'm basically back to where I was before the transplant. The doctors were right when they said I was living on borrowed time."

Manya puts the plate in front of Yael and sits down on the chair next to her. The small square table is squeezed into the corner so when they are all not eating, two of the chairs are pushed up against the wall. The tightness of the space makes Yael feel even more anxious.

"I don't know if I can go through this again."

"You have a child now, Yael." Manya speaks firmly and in an even tone. "It's not about you anymore. You need another transplant."

"How could I have been so selfish?" Yael whispers softly. "I never should have had a baby, especially without a husband. This is so unfair to Tikva."

Manya lifts up Yael's head, wipes away the tear dripping down her face, and hands her the forkful of eggs. "Eat."

They sit in silence, and although Yael is looking down, she can feel her mother's eyes on her. To avoid making eye contact, Yael keeps her eyes focused on her mother's hands. Her knobby knuckles protrude from the thin skin, which is speckled with dark spots. She knows her mother's palms are covered with calluses from years of working at the restaurant. As a young girl, Yael used to love rubbing her finger over the rough parts, but now she feels sad that at age seventy-five her mother still has to work so hard.

Yael scrapes the plate clean with her fork, and Manya quickly grabs it and puts it in the sink. "Thank you, *Ema*. You know, you don't need to wait on me hand and foot. You do that all day at work. You deserve a rest."

Manya washes the pan and wipes down the counter. "Not a word of this to *Abba*," she says. "He worries about you night and day."

"Where is *Abba*, anyway?" Yael is used to her father being in and out of the apartment, but by nine at night he's usually home, getting ready for bed. At eighty-one, he wakes up at the crack of dawn and generally doesn't stay up late at night.

"He had to drive Hindy Weiss somewhere," says Manya.

"This late at night?" Yael is incredulous. "He's an old man, he needs to sleep."

"Apparently the bulk store was offering a special *Motzei-Shabbat* sale on paper goods and she needed to stock up for *Pesach*."

Yael rolls her eyes. "She doesn't think about others, only about how to make life easier on herself."

"It's okay, don't get so mad," says Manya. "Hindy's not a bad person. She's just overwhelmed with her life. She has a lot of mouths to feed on a regular day, and *Pesach* is a week-long holiday of hard work for a religious woman."

"Well, I think she takes advantage," retorts Yael. "It was Yaakov's grandfather who brought *Abba* to Israel, not Hindy's, yet she's the one who calls for rides all the time."

"Enough, Yael." Manya holds up her hand. "Nothing will ever be too much for the Weiss family. *Abba* can never repay the debt. And anyway, you know he loves to drive his taxi."

Yael nods her head. Her father never seems happier than when behind the wheel of his old black Mercedes sedan. He has his beaded seat cover to ease the pain of sitting for hours, his favorite radio stations preset (although he listens to the news ninety-nine percent of the time), and his stash of lemon sucking candies in the glove compartment. "Srulik Glassman could talk to a doorknob," is what everyone says about him, and it's true. Her father loves meeting people, and he makes friends everywhere he goes.

"I need to go to sleep. Tell *Abba* I'm sorry I didn't wait up for him." Yael puts her hands on the table and pushes herself out of the chair. Manya wraps her arms around Yael's frail, bony body and hugs her tightly.

"*Layla Tov*," Manya says, kissing Yael on her forehead. "Sleep well."

Lying in her childhood bed, with Tikva just an arm's length away, Yael gazes at her sleeping daughter breathing rhythmically, and offers a silent prayer thanking God for giving her a healthy child. She isn't a religious person, but who else can she be grateful to for sparing her daughter from this terrible disease? She feels sad for her parents, who live as if they, too, are sick. Yael is their only child, and everything they do seems to revolve around her.

When Yael was diagnosed, the average lifespan for a person with CF was twenty-nine. Her parents sought out every new medication, treatment, and breathing therapy. They were determined Yael would be the miracle patient. Didn't God owe them at least that after all they suffered in the Holocaust? Luckily, until she started high school, her case was mild. Even so, her parents treated her as if she were fragile. They arranged their work schedules so she would never be home alone. Although most children in Israel walk to school alone or with friends, her parents always accompanied her.

As a teenager, Yael pushed back. She fought with her parents to let her be more independent, to go out late with friends, to sleep over at friends' homes. Whether it was acting more recklessly and not following medical protocol, or just the disease catching up with her, Yael's hospitalizations increased to three times a year, sometimes for a month at a time. She was forced to file for a medical exemption from the army, which, because it's mandatory for all Israelis, is a rite of passage that she was sad to miss out on. By her mid-twenties, Yael's condition had deteriorated so badly that she was listed for a double lung transplant, and miraculously, she received a new pair of lungs at twenty-six.

Yael fluffs up her pillows to keep her head elevated, inserts the clear tubes of the cannula into her nose, and turns the knob on the small tank of oxygen by her bed to release the flow. She doesn't need the oxygen all throughout the day—yet—but she sleeps better with it. She closes her eyes and tries to shut the noise in her head. Her brain is crowded with conflicting feelings of gratitude and resentment, happiness and anger. How lucky she was to have gotten a double lung transplant nine years ago, and to have lived for a few years magically believing she would always be a healthy person. To have traveled, fallen in love, had a baby. And yet...how cruel it was, to tease her with those years, to let her pretend she could have a normal life when it was certain the reprieve would not last forever.

The doctors had told Yael that transplants usually last about six years, and then, despite the powerful immunosuppressive drugs she was taking, her body would eventually fight back against the foreign lungs and reject them. This "chronic rejection" would ultimately lead to the lungs failing, and, unless she had a second transplant, to her death.

Yael opens her eyes and stares at the ceiling. The glow-in-the-dark star stickers she had placed there as a child still remain, and she tries to remember the names of the constellations. The universe is infinite, she thinks. I'm one tiny piece, and life on this Earth is short—but maybe somewhere else, it's not. This thought calms her.

Tikva suddenly snorts loudly and rolls over. Yael turns to look at her, and snaps out of her metaphysical reverie.

"*Ema*," whispers Tikva.

"Yes, *booba*."

"Can you lie with me?" Tikva scooches over to make room for Yael.

Yael's heart aches. She reaches down to turn off the oxygen flow and pulls the cannula out of her nose. She climbs into Tikva's bed and pulls her close, burying her head in Tikva's hair. Tikva wraps her arms around Yael. "I love you," she murmurs.

Yael kisses Tikva on the forehead. She feels a tight knot in her chest. Her poor child knows exactly what's going on, despite her attempts to keep things lighthearted. How could she not? Yael was just in the hospital for a month—that must have been terrifying for Tikva. She can't give her any reassurances about the future, and that's terrible for a child. Tikva needs therapy, she decides, and I need a miracle.

***

"ALLO! WHERE ARE MY beauties?" Srulik's voice booms as he bounces into the apartment. His short, wiry body is still as full of energy as a teenager's. Only the sparse hair on the sides of his head and his mustache, now all white, belie his age.

"Shhh! Srulik, *mah pitom*? What are you doing, shouting at the top of your lungs? Yael and Tiki are already asleep!" Manya admonishes him while at the same time turning on the kettle to make him a cup of tea.

"Asleep already? It's only nine o'clock. They must have had a wild day."

"No, Srulik, they didn't." Manya shakes her head sadly and purses her thin lips so they form a tight line. "Tiki went for a playdate in the morning and then watched TV the rest of the day, and Yael sat on the balcony with her sketching pads and took two naps."

A look of fear flashes across Srulik's face, and he squints his gray eyes, but then he smiles. "Sounds like a great day of relaxation—just what *Shabbat* is for! I'm sorry I missed it, but I drove Father Severin home from his shift at the hospital. It's damned unfair that those *haredim* run Jerusalem and don't allow buses to run on *Shabbat*, but it's good for the taxi business."

"You make no sense. You just drove one of those damned *haredim* and you also don't let anyone pay!"

"Let's not rehash this again, my dear," Srulik chuckles. "The kettle is boiling."

"How is Hindy?" Manya gives Srulik a glass mug of peppermint tea and sits next to him at the kitchen table.

"I think something is wrong, but I don't know what," says Srulik. "She's always very high-strung, but now she is even more anxious than usual. I could hear her yelling at the cashier from my car when one of the bags ripped."

"*Pesach* is a lot of work for the *haredim*. They keep the rules of the holiday even more than anyone—they probably clean every nook and cranny in the house to make sure there's not even one bread crumb."

Srulik shakes his head. "No, it's not that. I've known her for too long. I call Yaakov every Friday before *Shabbat,* but he never says anything. You know, Leah, their oldest, she still isn't married. But the second one already has a baby."

"So maybe that's what's bothering Hindy," says Manya. "You're only as happy as your unhappiest child."

Srulik stares into his mug. "I wish we could find a husband for Yael."

Manya shakes her head and takes the empty cup out of Srulik's hand. "That's not Yael's problem, and you know it."

Srulik slumps in his chair and the corners of his normally smiling mouth droop. Manya pats his hand. "Yael was listed for the transplant two months ago, so hopefully it will be soon."

"She's too low on the list," says Srulik.

"We have to look at it as a blessing that she's still healthy enough to have a low LAS (lung allocation score)," says Manya. "Anyway, there's nothing we can do about that."

"Not exactly..." Srulik paces the length of the kitchen. "When Yael was last hospitalized, I put in a call to Ruvi."

Ruvi, or Reuven Rivlin, is the former President of the State of Israel, and he grew up on Bialik Street in Beit Hakerem, across the way from Srulik. His wife, Nechama, suffered from pulmonary fibrosis and received a lung transplant from a drowning victim a few years ago.

"Okay, so you called Ruvi, *nu*, why is that a big announcement?" Manya asks.

"Because I asked him to work some magic to increase Yael's LAS so that she will be eligible for the next available pair of lungs," Srulik whispers.

"You can't do that, Srulik, it's illegal and immoral!" Manya's lips are pursed tight and she is straining not to yell and wake Yael and Tikva. "This is not one of your silly white lies, little stretches of the truth. These are people's lives you're talking about!"

"Our daughter's life! Isn't she the most important person in the world?"

"To us, yes," says Manya. "But to another family, someone else is. Think about my boss David Sassoon—he's been waiting for a liver for nearly a year. He might die before it's his turn on the list. But that's God's decision, not ours."

Srulik pounds the kitchen table with his fist. "I'll be damned if I leave this up to God. Had people not lied about me, had I not lied about myself, I would have died with the rest of my family in the camps. God didn't help anyone."

Manya runs her fingers through her short, gray bob. She shuts her eyes and takes a deep breath. "It doesn't matter anyway; Ruvi will never break the law."

Srulik hangs his head. He looks pale. He grimaces as if in physical pain.

Manya pats him on the shoulder. "Yael is hanging in there. It was a cold and rainy winter, and the weather didn't agree with her. You'll see, spring is here and Yael's going to be okay."

Srulik shakes his head, looking less than hopeful. "From your mouth to God's ears."

***

O N SUNDAY MORNING, YAEL wakes up at five. She doesn't need to wake Tikva for two more hours, but she needs the time to do all of her medical treatments to help her get through the day. She tiptoes out of the room into the kitchen and pours herself a tall glass of water. Yael takes about fifty pills a day to help her to digest her food and to prevent further lung infections. She gulps the water a little too quickly and starts to cough. Quickly, she grabs a kitchen towel and tries to muffle herself, so her mother won't wake up.

Too late. Not even a minute later, Manya is in the kitchen, boiling the kettle.

"*Ema*, I'm fine," says Yael. "There's no reason for you to be up this early. The water just went down the wrong way."

"I was up anyway," says Manya. "Your father has been snoring terribly, and I can't sleep. But it's okay, it will give me time to watch my show."

Yael giggles. "*Ema*, I still can't believe you watch *The Bachelorette*! Of all the shows to be addicted to...it's shocking to me."

Manya tries to hide a smile. "It's quite a fascinating show. Very good insights into psychology. You know, I was almost a psychologist."

"Before I was born, and ruined your life," Yael says. "You had to sacrifice everything for me."

"*Chas V'Chalila!* God forbid!" Manya says. "Do you know what a miracle it was for us to have a child after surviving the Holocaust? Never, ever say you ruined my life."

"Okay, but I ruined your plans to become a psychologist."

"Who wants to spend all day with crazy people anyway?" Manya pours herself a cup of coffee and twists one of Yael's long, brown ringlets of hair around her finger. "You don't have to do the vest for the whole hour. I'll do the percussion for thirty minutes after you finish."

Yael normally spends two hours each morning inhaling medication through a nebulizer to help open her airways. While she has the blue pipe in her mouth, she also wears a black vibrating vest that helps to loosen and clear the mucus that accumulated in her lungs overnight. When her mother's arthritic hands aren't hurting too much, she spends about thirty minutes tapping Yael's chest and back, which is what she had to do when Yael was too young for the vest. Every few minutes she has to spit out globs of putrid, green mucus into a bucket.

"Okay, thank you *Ema*." Yael plugs in her headphones and listens to her favorite podcast, "Armchair Traveler," while she lets the equipment do its job so that she can breathe decently during the day. Before the transplant, she was matter-of-fact about these two wasted hours of her day. It was early in the morning, no one else was doing anything anyway, and she accepted it as a way to live a relatively normal life. The transplant not only freed her from being tethered to machines, but it also gave her more hours—better hours—to live as she wanted.

Yael tries listening to the walking tour of Lisbon, but she can't focus. All she can think about is how her lungs are failing, and she doesn't know if or how she will survive another lung transplant. What will happen to Tikva?

As if on cue, Tikva walks into the room. She is the spitting image of her father: a man named Max that Yael had a month-long fling with when she was visiting Berlin, six months after her lung transplant. Tikva is one of the tallest in her class, with blonde hair and gray-blue eyes. Her sturdy frame looks out of place with the thin and bony Glassman family, and especially compared to Yael, who is perpetually underweight. Only Tikva's deep dimples, identical to Yael's, bear a family resemblance. She is wearing a pink T-shirt with her school's emblem in a small circle above her chest, and black leggings with rainbows wrapping each ankle.

"*Booba*, what are you doing up this early?" Yael asks, quickly pressing the off button for the vest and spitting out the nebulizer tube. The steam from the inhaler lingers in the air for a moment, clouding Yael's face.

"I heard you and *Savta* talking and you woke me up!" Tikva replies, rubbing her eyes.

"I'm sorry. Well, now you have extra time before school, so how about some *choco*?"

Tikva licks her lips. Chocolate milk is her favorite. "Yes *Ema*!"

Manya pats the worn, brown chintz seat next to her. "Come watch my show with me. It's fascinating. Yael, finish what you were doing. I'll get Tiki her *choco*."

Tiki comes close to Yael. "*Ema*, are you okay?" She furrows her brow and peers closely at Yael's face. "Do you want me to do some tapping on your back for you?"

Yael's heart swells and constricts, all at once. She feels so lucky to have a sweet, caring daughter, and so awful that she is filling her life with worry.

"You're the most loveable, sweet girl in the whole world," says Yael, squeezing Tikva tightly. "I'm okay. *Savta* will do some tapping when I'm done with my vest, and then we'll go to school. Now go enjoy your *choco*."

Yael tries to resume her breathing therapy, but she feels a wave of sadness so strong that tears spring from her eyes without warning. Quickly, she goes into the bathroom and turns on the sink at full force, so neither Tikva nor her mother will hear her sniffling.

"You know there's a drought in Israel!" shouts Srulik, pounding on the door. "Shut the water!"

Yael bursts out laughing. There hasn't been a drought in Israel in years, but her father still issues his public service campaign not to waste water. The laughing makes her cough, and she waits a moment before opening the bathroom door, so she won't frighten her sensitive father. "*Boker Tov, Abba*. I hope we didn't wake you, too." Then she erupts in a coughing fit.

"Why are your eyes red?" Srulik's bushy eyebrows furrow, and he gives Yael a kiss on her forehead. "*Oy, mamale*, what's wrong?"

Yael feels the tears well up again. Since her latest bout of pneumonia, even the two hours of mucus release hasn't been enough, and by the afternoon, she needs to sit with her oxygen tank and take a nap. She's exhausted from the sheer effort of breathing. Thinking about the suffocating feeling fills her with anxiety and dread.

Srulik envelops her in a bear hug. Yael feels comforted like a little girl when he holds her like this. "I'd better finish the treatments so we can take Tiki to school."

Tikva shouts from the living room: "I can walk myself!"

"I know you can, but school is on the way to the Y. We'll drop you off there," says Yael, flatly. She hates herself for saying it and resents forcing Tikva to be bubble-wrapped just as Yael was as a child.

Before she and Tikva moved in with her parents, Yael allowed Tikva to walk by herself to school, to go to the corner market alone, even to ride the city buses without her. She relished giving her daughter the independence she never had as a young girl. The combination of Yael's illness with her parents' wartime trauma made them unable to leave her alone. Srulik arranged his hours driving a taxi so that he would be available when Manya was working at the restaurant. They were always by her side. She felt smothered by their overbearing presence, but even as a child, she understood they were only trying to protect her.

She remembered when she was nine years old, she was hospitalized for surgery to remove her adenoids and tonsils, which doctors thought would help with her breathing. She had to sleep in the hospital, and at that time, parents were not allowed to stay overnight. Srulik refused to leave Yael, and hid under her hospital bed, lying all night on the cold linoleum floor.

But Tikva is different. She's not sick, and Yael isn't a Holocaust survivor. There's no reason for extreme helicopter parenting. Yael realizes that her parents don't know any other way to take care of a child and worries what Tikva's life will be like if her parents become her guardians if Yael dies.

"I don't want to ride in *Saba*'s stinky car," whines Tikva.

"Hey! I just put in a new air freshener," says Srulik.

Tikva sticks out her tongue.

"And if we hurry, we can pop into the bakery on the way to school."

"Yay!"

"And I'll also bring you back your favorite *baklava* from the restaurant," says Manya, gently pushing Tiki off the couch. "But now, can everyone be quiet so I can watch my show?"

***

T HE LIMESTONE FACADE OF the Jerusalem YMCA blends in with all the other buildings in the city; it's a local ordinance that all architecture must use the white-peach stone. The Y sits in the center of the city, opposite the stately King David Hotel, which is the most luxurious, historic, and important hotel in the country. The bell tower differentiates the Y from its surroundings, and was once the tallest structure in Jerusalem, when it was built nearly a century ago. In the sunlight of this warm Sunday morning in April, the stone glints and sparkles, mesmerizing Yael even though she has seen it a million times.

The Y symbolically unifies Jerusalem's diverse population. Muslim, Christian, Jewish, Israeli, Arab, international...there are people of every size, shape, and color at the Y. Political and religious differences are left outside the building, or at least it seems so to Yael. Perhaps that's why she's so comfortable here. In a weird way, it reminds Yael of the only good part of the hospital, where, because people are stripped down to their bare humanity, both literally and figuratively, they generally are kind to one another.

Srulik drives up King David Street and passes the main entrance to the Y, which is studded with multiple arched windows and fronted by beautiful gardens. He turns the car down a small cobblestone alley meant only for pedestrians, so he can drop Yael off on the side entrance closest to the pool.

"Usual place, usual time?" Srulik asks. "Or should I come earlier?"

"I'm okay, *Abba*," replies Yael. Her voice is raspy from the coughing jag this morning. "The swimming will be good for me. I'll see you in the back garden later. Win your game!"

"*Betach*. I always do," says Srulik. He reverses the car and heads towards his long-standing Sunday morning backgammon game.

Yael enters through the sliding doors and waves hello to Nura, the albino Arab woman who sits behind the check-in desk. When Nura first started working at the Y a few months ago, Yael immediately recognized her albinism from her translucent skin and her white eyebrows and eyelashes, even though her head was covered with a hijab. Yael wondered how it felt to be so visibly different, even though albinism isn't a terrible disease like cystic fibrosis. But Yael's illness is invisible. She doesn't look sick on the outside, except that she is very skinny, and some people think she is anorexic. She never knows how to broach the topic with Nura, so she just says good morning, scans her membership chip, and passes through the turnstile.

"*Boker Tov*, Yael," says Elad, the muscular, young security guard, waving to her from his perch on a wooden stool by the front window.

Yael greets all of the regular staff and guests, feeling a sense of calm come over her. The Y has been her special place ever since she was a child. Her parents sent her to the *gan* here, and she loved being in kindergarten with children of diverse backgrounds. Even once she switched to a local neighborhood elementary school, she still came to the Y for swimming lessons.

The pool at the Y was for many years the only indoor swimming pool in the country. Even though the mild Middle Eastern climate doesn't usually include very cold weather, the temperatures can drop low enough in Jerusalem for occasional snow flurries. The original pool, no longer in use, is deep in the dark recesses of the basement. The new pool has three-story-high glass walls, so even indoors Yael feels the bright warmth of the near-constant Israeli sunshine.

In the locker room, Yael sees the old women who come when the pool opens, at six a.m., and are now still leisurely blow-drying their hair and chatting with each other as they pack their bags. "*Boker Tov*, Yael," says Claudia, a woman in her eighties who is the unofficial leader of the swim pack. None of them are friends outside of the Y—they don't call or text each other, and they mostly only know each other's first names—but they consider themselves a group, nevertheless. They are the early birds, while Yael is still part of the parents' post-drop-off group, which she joined when Tikva attended *gan* at the Y.

"Hi Claudia," says Yael. "How's the water today?"

"Oh, it's beautiful," says Claudia. "The perfect temperature. And the sun is shining through and creating shimmering rainbows on the water."

Yael smiles. "You make it sound very inviting! I can't wait to get in." She struggles to lift off her shirt, erupting in another coughing fit.

"Are you okay, Yael?" Claudia comes closer and puts a hand on Yael's back. Claudia and the other regulars know that Yael's coughs are related to CF, and not because of a cold or flu. Until a few years ago, no one suspected anything about her health, but as her body has been more determinedly rejecting her new lungs, she has had a few episodes of uncontrolled wheezing and coughing in the pool, which prompted her to reveal her health situation to her pool friends.

"I'm okay," Yael sputters. "Just got something caught in my throat." Breathing fast, she sits down on the wooden bench. She ties her long curls into a low ponytail, then tucks the ponytail into a blue swim cap. She hopes Claudia will leave, so she won't have to talk to her anymore. She just wants to get in the water and forget about everything for a while.

Yael started swimming when she was very little, because the doctors told her parents that swimming would help to increase her lung capacity and expel mucus. She became an excellent swimmer, competing on her high school team despite missing practice frequently for infections. The swimming pool was her refuge; the only place she was truly on her own. Even though her parents waited for her in the lobby, Yael was free in the water. She could swim fast, without someone telling her: "Slow down, you might fall!"

Yael puts her towel down on the diving block at the head of the left-most lane, the one closest to the lifeguard, Walid. This lane is usually open for her, and if someone else happens to be in the lane, Walid makes him move into another one of the ten lanes. After rescuing Yael a few months ago when she started wheezing terribly and didn't have the strength to get out of the pool, Walid has become very protective of Yael. Maybe even a little too protective, she thinks.

"*Boker Tov*, Yael," says Walid, waving enthusiastically. "You feeling good?"

"Yes, Walid. I'm feeling good."

Claudia was right, Yael thinks, as she eases herself into the pool. The water is perfect today. The sunlight bounces around the room, and Yael makes swirls in the water with her fingers spread wide as she tries to relax. Swimming is still her mental release; the forced sensory deprivation of being under the water is the best cure for her anxiety.

She dunks, then pushes off the wall and starts swimming breaststroke, her favorite stroke. Up, out, together go her legs, as her arms pull her torso out of the water. It's a twenty-five-meter pool, half-Olympic size. When she was healthy, she could swim sixty-four laps—a mile—without stopping. Since she got out of the hospital two months ago, she can barely do ten laps. And today, she fears she won't even be able to do that.

It feels like an eternity until Yael makes it to the other end of the pool. She is exhausted from the effort, breathing heavily even though she swam very slowly. She tries to take short, shallow breaths so she won't cough. Looking up, she sees Walid watching her carefully. She pretends to adjust her goggles; she doesn't want him jumping in and "rescuing" her again. He's a sweet guy. He was only doing his job. But she didn't need the embarrassment, the rush of EMTs, and all the gawking onlookers.

She decides to swim backstroke. Maybe if her head is out of the water, she can breathe more shallowly and continuously. Fluttering her feet and working her arms like windmills alongside her, Yael starts swimming. She stares at the ceiling, trying to keep to a straight line. She doesn't swim backstroke very often, and she keeps veering to the side and hitting the thick, plastic rope that separates her lane from the next. As she approaches the other end of the pool, she sees the banner of multicolored, triangular flags overhead, the reminder to back swimmers that they are approaching the wall. Regular backstrokers know to count their strokes when they see the flags. Yael guesses that she has nine strokes to the end, so she propels her arms, counting out loud, and then bang! Her head slams into the wall of the pool. She blacks out and sinks beneath the water.

***

M EANWHILE, AFTER SRULIK DROPS Yael off, he drives back up King David Street, one of the fanciest boulevards in the city. In addition to the Y, it hosts four luxury hotels, many art galleries, and a few car rental agencies. Just past the King David hotel, at the corner of Paul Emile Botta Street, is the Paz gas station, where Srulik meets his taxi buddies.

The men sit outside the station's Yellow Cafe on white plastic chairs surrounding two round tables. Behind one table is an outlet, and there's always a fight over who gets to sit there and charge his phone. Big plastic-wrapped bundles of large water bottles sit piled up on the ground next to them, and the men occasionally use them as extra seating, or as footrests. The curb is painted red and white to indicate no parking, but Srulik parks his car there, anyway. There's a Budget car rental across the street, and when their customer line snakes around the block, the taxi drivers walk over with their coffees and offer their services.

It's been like this for years, with a rotating cast of characters; Srulik comes regardless of who's there, stopping no matter what for his second coffee and to talk. He regales the younger drivers with stories from the past, of famous passengers, of a time before people could summon drivers with a smartphone app.

"*Boker Tov*, Gidi. Nachman. Eliezer. Zevi! *Mah Shlomcha*? It's been a long time." Srulik motions for the men to give him a seat. When only Zevi gets up, Srulik scowls at the others. "This is how you treat an old man?"

"Today you want to be an old man?" asks Gidi. He's quite old himself, about sixty, with dark skin and a full head of salt and pepper hair. "Yesterday you told me you were as strong as when you were twenty-five."

"Well, today I feel my age," says Srulik, plopping down on the chair with a loud sigh. "I'm eighty-one and my mind is troubled, my heart is in pain."

"What a poet!" Gidi laughs, but Srulik doesn't smile.

"Srulik, is something really wrong?" Gidi asks.

"You don't listen," complains Srulik. "For weeks, I've been telling you about my daughter. She's still sick. It eats me up inside."

"I'm sorry," says Gidi. "But she's not getting worse, is she?"

Srulik shakes his head. "Not really. I don't think so. But she's not better." He waves his hand in front of his face. "Never mind. I shouldn't have said anything. Come, let's play. It will do me good, take my mind off things."

The men take out two backgammon boards, one for each table. They will play round-robin games for hours until one of them has to go back on his driving shift. Srulik is the only one who doesn't drive his taxi regularly anymore; he generally only gives free rides to friends and family who don't have cars. The men leave the small radio permanently tuned to Galgalatz, the station operated by the Israel Defense Forces, for the most up-to-date news and traffic.

Srulik rolls the dice and is about to move his pieces when the radio's music program is interrupted: "This is Roni Saban. We have reports of a terrorist attack. A bus has exploded on Route One, just outside the entrance to Jerusalem. At least eight people are dead, and many others wounded. The highway is closed in both directions."

The men stop their games and sit silently, heads bent together over the radio. There is an eruption of wailing ambulances and whirring helicopters.

"I thought we were done with bus bombings," says Nachman. "The second Intifada is long over, no?"

"Shhh!"

An ambulance races up King David Street and turns into the big semi-circle entrance of the YMCA.

Srulik jumps out of his chair and races across the street.

"Srulik, where are you going?"

***

A FEW HOURS LATER, Yael is sitting in a hospital bed on the third floor of Shaare Zedek Medical Center. The room is all beige: the paint on the walls, the linoleum tiles on the floor, the formica on the cabinets, the plastic side chairs. Yael thinks the blandness is meant to relax patients, but it adds to her feeling of claustrophobia and anxiety. The walls feel as if they are closing in on her, despite the large three-paned window.

Her mother has just arrived, after picking Tikva up from school and dropping her at a friend's house for an after-school playdate. Srulik is pacing back and forth, his hands jingling coins in his pocket as he walks.

Her parents must feel just as trapped as she does, Yael realizes. They've given their whole lives for her, and yet, it's not enough. They can't save her. This is a nightmare for all of them. She lies back on the bed and closes her eyes.

"Srulik, *mah pitom*! Stop that crazy noise, it's giving Yael a headache," scolds Manya. She walks over to the bed from the doorway, where she has been standing guard since she arrived, peeking her head outside every few minutes to check for the doctor.

"*Ema*, it's fine. Hospitals are so noisy with all the beeping machines I don't even notice it anymore," says Yael.

"Speaking of machines, why aren't you hooked up to anything?" Manya looks at the dark monitors next to the bed.

"Because there's nothing wrong," says Yael, exasperatedly. "I hit my head on the wall in the pool and I blacked out for about three seconds. But Walid panicked and called the ambulance, and now I'm here."

"The emergency room was a *balagan* because of the bombing. Drorit was the intake nurse, and once she saw that Yael was okay, she just moved Yael straight upstairs into a room for observation," says Srulik. "We're supposed to wait for Dr. Starr to come give her the all-clear."

"I heard about the bombing when I was at work," says Manya, clucking her tongue. "Awful. I thought the days of suicide bombings were over."

"Me too," says Yael. "It makes me so scared." She shivers and pulls the blanket up higher on her chest.

Manya goes over to Yael and reaches for her hand. "Your hand is freezing, and your lips are turning blue."

"*Ema*, I did not have a breathing attack." Although as she is speaking, her breathing is becoming heavier, and her lips are very slightly tinged blue.

"Maybe not, but you don't look very good. Srulik, go find the doctor. This is crazy."

"No, wait, *Abba*," Yael tries to even her breathing, and she sits up straight. "*Abba, Ema*, please. I've been doing a lot of thinking lately and I want to talk to both of you."

"Now?" Srulik shakes his head. "Yael, this is not a time to talk and waste your energy. You have to rest and get better."

"*Abba*, I'm not sick!" Yael shouts, and then erupts into a coughing jag. She motions to her mother to pass her a cup, and she hacks up a large blob of smelly green mucus and spits into the cup. "I don't need to rest, but I do need to talk to you."

"Well, let me just check down the hall for a minute to see if Dr. Starr is anywhere," says Manya, heading to the doorway.

"I swear, *Ema,* if you don't sit down right now, I'm going to scream," says Yael. Her face is straining with the effort.

Srulik and Manya sit on the two plastic chairs by the window and look expectantly at Yael.

"I think we need to talk about a plan for Tiki."

"Well, I took her to a playdate and either *Abba* or I will pick her up and bring her home for dinner," says Manya. "Do they think you're going to have to stay in the hospital overnight? It's not a problem—we'll take care of her."

"No, *Ema*, it is a problem," says Yael softly. "I'm not talking about today. I'm talking about tomorrow, and the next day, and the day after that." She pauses, and whispers, "If I'm not around, I'm not sure it's the best thing for Tiki to live with you two."

Manya looks startled for a minute, then stands up. "Well, I'm going to find the doctor."

"*Ema*, please tell me you are listening to me," says Yael. "This is not like the restaurant, where you can pretend you didn't hear someone's order because you think they should eat something else. This is my daughter's life."

"And you are OUR DAUGHTER," roars Srulik, standing right at the edge of Yael's bed. "Don't tell me I survived the Holocaust just to have my one and only child die. I refuse to talk about Tikva and who will take care of her. YOU will take care of her. You will get another transplant, and YOU WILL LIVE. And if you need a third transplant in ten years, you'll get another one then, too."

Just at that moment, an overweight male orderly dressed in green scrubs and black sneakers comes in to mop the floor and take out the garbage. He pulls his large, yellow bucket and sets it in a corner.

"*Mah Pitom!*" shouts Srulik. "Get out of here now, you *nudnik*! Can't you see we're in the middle of a serious conversation?"

The orderly reddens and shuffles out of the room.

"Now, where were we?" Srulik asks. "You were giving up on your life?" His hands are shaking, and his face is beet red.

Yael can't say what she's thinking: that she doesn't want Tiki to live with two very old people who worry about everything. It would shatter them. "I just worry that it will be too much for you to handle, taking care of Tiki if I'm not able to."

Manya looks at Yael and purses her lips. She nods her head the tiniest bit. "Don't worry about us. We are strong. And Tiki is an easy child. We'll be fine."

Yael tries not to cry but she can't rid herself of feelings of self-pity for being sick; regret for not thinking things through before she recklessly had a child without a partner; resentment for not having siblings or cousins to lean on; and fear of what might happen. She's sinking down a hole quickly and has nothing to grab onto.

Manya lifts Yael's chin and wipes her tears with a tissue. "You're a good mother, Yael. No one plans to be sick."

Yael sniffles, coughs up more green mucus, spits it into a tissue. "I shouldn't have had a baby."

"It was the best thing you ever did," Manya says. "For you, for us, and for Tikva. She forced you to take care of things by yourself, which is something we never did."

Yael looks at her mother with surprise.

Manya smiles. "Even though I didn't become a psychologist, it doesn't mean I don't know things."

Srulik takes out some of the coins from his pocket and stacks them on the tray next to Yael's bed. "Give these to the orderly the next time he comes in."

Yael reaches her arms up to her parents. "Give me a hug, both of you."

She embraces Srulik and Manya, one on each side of her. Srulik pulls away first and wipes the tears from his eyes.

"Do me a favor, please go. It's late. *Ema*, go back to work. I know David is still out sick and Rachel needs you to help with the dinner shift. *Abba*, go pick up Tiki and give her dinner. I'm sure Dr. Starr will be here soon, and I'll call you when I can leave. He probably won't even want me to stay overnight."

Srulik and Manya reluctantly go, and Yael falls asleep.

A short while later, Dr. Starr comes into the room and taps her shoulder.

"I'm sorry to wake you, Yael, but I need to check on you."

Yael rubs her eyes. "It's fine. I wasn't sleeping."

"I hear that you couldn't breathe while you were swimming and so then you knocked into the wall of the pool?"

"No, that's not how it happened," Yael snaps, exasperated. "I didn't count my strokes properly and banged my head into the wall. I blacked out for three seconds, but everyone freaked out."

Dr. Starr runs his fingers through his short black hair. "Well, better safe than sorry. I saw they did a CT scan, and it was fine, but let's check on your breathing, too, since you're here."

He scrolls down his iPad. "Looks like we listed you for a second transplant about two months ago. It's a little early, but with repeaters like you, we need to get you new lungs before you get too sick. Right now, it seems the only problem is with the lungs, so that's a good thing. How often are you using oxygen?"

"Usually a few hours a day."

"Okay, that's not too bad," says Dr. Starr.

"And most of the night."

"Oh." He slicks his hair back again with his fingers. "Well, sounds like you're not far from needing oxygen full time. We can repeat the six-minute walk test and do another bronchoscopy, but I'm not sure those are necessary. It seems like a wait-and-see game."

When Yael came in for a routine checkup, she would often tune out what Dr. Starr was saying and fawn over at him, wondering: How is his hair always so perfectly in line? Does he get a haircut every day? Why is his facial stubble always the same thickness? Today, Yael barely pays attention to what he looks like. She is listening to his breath. She doesn't hear it. There are no gasps in between sentences. No pauses between words to cough, or to spit out mucus. There's a confidence in his voice, a cadence to his words. He doesn't talk as if he's scared that he'll start coughing or wheezing. He trusts in his lungs.

"Dr. Starr, sorry to interrupt you, but do you really think a second transplant is the right thing for me?"

Dr. Starr looks startled. "What do you mean?"

"Well, won't my body just reject these lungs, too?" Yael feels herself shivering. She pulls the sheet up to her chin. Dr. Starr quickly steps into the hall to get another blanket, which he drapes over her.

"Listen, your first transplant was a major success," he says. "Your lungs lasted almost three years longer than the average. We'll continue to give you excellent care, and hopefully you'll have another successful time and many healthy years ahead."

"Do you think it will go as smoothly as last time?"

"I'm not a fortune teller, Yael. Obviously, with a second transplant, we're looking at a harder road than before. There's scar tissue buildup from the first operation. It can take longer to cut out the lungs. Sometimes that means a lot of bleeding, and that the donor lungs may be out of the body for longer than ideal."

"But even if it works, it's still just an average of six years, right? Then I'll get chronic rejection again and I'll start to have shortness of breath and I'll be right back at square one?" Yael twists the corner of the blanket. She can feel her heart beating fast from the effort it's taking to speak so much. She's so tired, she just wants to sleep.

"Well, yes, but six years is six years," says Dr. Starr. "You faced an incredibly challenging disease with grit and grace, and it's paid off. Look how much you've accomplished these last nine years."

Yael nods. "I traveled, I had a baby, I got my own apartment, I got a job. I was normal."

"So, there you go. But you do sound a little short of breath. How about you rest for a bit, and I'll come back in a few hours, and we can do those two tests?"

"I get out of breath now, just taking a shower," Yael whispers. "My parents have to do everything for me: cook, clean, do laundry, take care of my daughter. I'm not an independent adult."

Dr. Starr looks at her. "You're in the late stages of chronic rejection, Yael. It's hard. And unfortunately, it's a reasonable expectation that you will get to a point where you will have to be put on a ventilator. It can help buy you time."

"I can't go on a ventilator again!" Yael feels her heart fluttering wildly. "It was horrible. Even while I was sedated, I felt like I was drowning."

"We can try to increase the sedation."

"No! And then what? I'm truly a vegetable?"

"Listen Yael," warns Dr. Starr. "Even if you avoid a ventilator before the transplant, you know that you'll need to be on one for at least a few days afterward."

Yael nods her head. She's trying to listen, but she's also thinking about cuddling in bed this morning with Tikva. What's the right thing for her to do? To let her daughter get even more attached to her, or to try to have Tiki acclimate to a life without her while she's still so young and resilient?

"You know what it takes to be a successful transplant recipient. It's not all automatic. You have to put in the work," continues Dr. Starr. "You were really determined and excited last time, and that's part of why you were so successful and why things went smoothly. I need you to do a major attitude adjustment if this is going to work, okay?"

He tells Yael about a patient of his who had post-operative depression and anxiety and how it led to problems with ventilation even though the lungs themselves were fine because the patient couldn't inflate and deflate his new lungs and so had to stay on a mechanical ventilator.

"He couldn't handle the work," said Dr. Starr. "Basically, he wanted to die. It took a lot of yelling and screaming by his wife and handholding by me to get him back into it."

Yael imagines herself lying in a hospital bed again, attached to tubes and wires, unable to speak or to move. It was so hard the last time. She's not sure if she can do it again.

"Be honest with me," pleads Yael. "Tikva is eight years old. I know I won't make it to her wedding, but would I be able to live until she's eighteen, long enough with a second transplant that she wouldn't need a guardian?"

"Only God knows the answer to that," answers Dr. Starr. "But statistically, it's a long shot."

Yael thinks about all of the people on her CF support chat group. CF patients can never meet one another in person, because they are too susceptible to infecting one another with their bacteria-ridden sputum. Their internet connection has been a lifeline for her over the years. She can truly relate to these people. She closes her eyes, and thinks, if I get this second transplant, someone else might not get their first.

"It feels very selfish of me to get a second transplant," she admits. "I had another chance at life. Why should I get yet another? Because I'm the only child of Holocaust survivors?"

"Maybe," replies Dr. Starr. "We do have special dispensations in the army for kids who are only children."

He takes Yael's hands into his. "Listen, Yael, survivor guilt is very normal with organ transplantation. It's an emotional minefield. But you are a good candidate for a second transplant, and you do deserve it. Maybe it would help to speak to a therapist to help you deal with all these feelings."

Yael pulls her hands away. "I don't want to talk about these feelings or even have these feelings at all...I can't. It's too hard."

Dr. Starr touches her cheek tenderly.

She turns her head away and murmurs softly, "What if I tell you I won't be compliant with the medications after surgery? Won't that discount me from being eligible?"

"What are you saying, Yael?" Dr. Starr raises his voice. "I'm shocked, and frankly...a little annoyed. Our team is going to do the best to take care of you, but you are not going to disgrace the donor—who will have died too young—by wasting a pair of lungs."

"I don't know if I can go through it all again," says Yael. "Take me off the list."

Dr. Starr smacks his hand on his head and strides to the doorway. "Maybe you did get knocked in the head a little too hard today. I'll come back later."

He pauses by the door. "You know, just a few floors below you people are dying from their injuries in the bus bombing today. They won't all get a second chance. But you might. Don't throw that away."

Yael doesn't answer. She closes her eyes and tries to sleep.

***

A FEW HOURS LATER, Dr. Starr comes bounding into the room. "Yael, I hope you've changed your tune, because you're not going to believe this: We have a set of lungs."

Kidney Two

I N THE SEVEN YEARS since Hoda Ibrahim opened her beauty salon, she has never styled a bride's hair. She is renowned in her East Jerusalem neighborhood for her utmost discretion and impeccable style. Beneath her hijab, her thick brunette hair is streaked with golden highlights, and her almond-shaped, brown eyes are lined with kohl. Yet as a young widow, an unspoken superstition keeps wedding parties away.

"It's ridiculous that brides don't come here. *Alhamdulillah*, you are the finest stylist in town," says Yasmin Al-Hashimi, Hoda's cousin and business partner. She slams the bookkeeping notebook closed, jingling the thin stack of gold bangles on her arm. "A wedding party would give us more money in a day than we make in a week."

"It's true," Hoda replies. "*Inshallah* our luck will change soon."

"*Inshallah*." Yasmin looks across the room at Hoda, who is taking inventory of the metal supply cabinet. "But if things don't improve, Hoda, if we can't turn a profit, we may have to think about closing the salon."

Hoda doesn't turn around. She can feel Yasmin's piercing green eyes as she tries to measure how swollen Hoda's ankles are today. The early April heatwave is making her even more swollen than usual. She's aching to get off the step stool, but doesn't want Yasmin watching when she climbs down.

"It's backbreaking work," says Yasmin, the furrows in her brow deepening. "And if you don't get a kidney soon..."

Hoda grabs onto the stool, gritting her teeth as she steps down as gracefully as she can. Her shoes make a loud clomp as they hit the floor. She doesn't need Yasmin to remind her. She's been managing her polycystic kidney disease for five years. But last summer the symptoms worsened. No longer could Hoda write off the swelling in her feet and ankles from standing all day in the salon; nor the loss of her appetite, the itchiness, the muscle cramps. Dr. Applebaum had warned if she didn't get a transplant soon, she would have to go on dialysis.

It's something she wants desperately to avoid, both to keep her disease private (only her family knows), and because, as the only parent and only source of income, she can't afford to be tethered to a machine for hours every week. The salon is her lifeline.

"We're nearly out of the keratin treatments," Hoda says, ignoring Yasmin's comments. "And we need more disposable gloves and paper towels."

Yasmin pushes her chair away from the reception desk, walks across the room, and takes Hoda's hands in hers. She tries to look into Hoda's eyes, but Hoda averts her gaze, hoping Yasmin won't notice their slight yellowing. Hoda is nearly a head taller than her older cousin.

Yasmin cranes her head. "If you don't want to talk about your health, at least tell me you're going to stop dating and just pick a man and get married. That would certainly help things around here."

Hoda laughs and gives Yasmin a hug. She is used to her cousin's bluntness. Yasmin is just old enough to tell Hoda what to do, but not so much older that she can enforce her will. Even so, Hoda admits, most of the time Yasmin has good ideas. Ahmed died when Hoda was just thirty-one, and with two young sons, she felt completely lost. It was Yasmin's suggestion to open the salon. Seven years later, Hoda is pleasantly surprised the arrangement is working out so well.

The Be-You-Beauty Salon is just a short walk from Hoda's apartment. It's a small shop, on a dusty street with a corner grocer, a restaurant, and a dental clinic. The street lies within the shadow of the border wall, which the Israeli government built twenty years ago to seal itself off from the Palestinian territories.

The wall is about twenty-five feet high, built of concrete graffitied with murals commemorating the *Nakba*, and plastered with posters of Arabs who died fighting the Israelis. Atop the wall is a five-foot crown of barbed wire that holds many stray plastic bags and crushed soda cans. Apartment buildings are so close to both sides of the wall that neighbors on high floors can still see one another and smell each other's cooking. The meaty smoke from one family's *shawarma* mingles with the smell of eggplant frying in oil for another's *maqloubeh*.

Inside the salon, Hoda tries to forget about the wall. The windows are shuttered, in accordance with Muslim law, so that women will not be seen inside with their heads uncovered. There are three sinks and three styling stations with mirrors, although Hoda is the only one who cuts and colors hair. Yasmin does the shampooing, the sweeping, the bookkeeping, and reception. Faded *Vogue* magazine covers adorn the walls, and there is a small table in the back with piles of chiffon scarves for sale.

The shutters don't keep out the loud car honking from the road, so to drown out the din, Hoda and Yasmin play on loop the songs of Umm Kulthum, the Egyptian folk singer for whom the street is named. By the end of the day, Hoda's head is pounding from the noise, but she is happy. With its music, boisterous laughter, and safe intimacy, the salon has become sort of a women's club. They share recipes, offer parenting advice, and commiserate about the water shortage. She hears whispered confessions of abusive husbands, difficult in-laws, disobedient children. Hoda enjoys the friendships and camaraderie, especially when she coaxes off a woman's hijab and sees a glint in her client's eye. "Should we go for purple streaks?" she'll ask, with a wink.

Today, however, Hoda's pain is worsening, and she aches to lie down. She pulls away from Yasmin and reaches over to turn off the radio. It is just after three o'clock on Sunday, but the salon has been empty for over an hour.

"Why don't we close early today, Hoda?" Yasmin asks. "It's been a slow day, and you look like you could use a rest."

"I guess we could," says Hoda. "But I don't need to rest. Maybe I'll just take a quick shower and then I'll call Srulik and ask him to take me to the store so we can restock."

"Ah, the famous Srulik!" Yasmin chuckles. "Only you would have a Jew taxi driver at your beck and call. It's one of those things I love most about you, Hoda. You don't care what anyone thinks."

Hoda shrugs and gives Yasmin a sheepish grin. Nearly twenty years ago, Srulik Glassman was driving east on Route 60 from Central Jerusalem to the predominantly Jewish Pisgat Ze'ev neighborhood, just one exit ahead of the Arab village of Beit Hanina, when his car hit a pothole and broke down. Ahmed happened to be driving on the road just behind Srulik and offered help. He told Srulik that he was a mechanic with his own shop and could replace his broken axle for a fraction of the normal cost. Srulik agreed and was so pleased with the service and the price that he began to bring his fellow taxi buddies to Ahmed's and his brother Mohammed's shop for repairs. Years of working together created a deep familiarity, if not an actual friendship, between the men. When Ahmed died, Hoda was not surprised when Srulik called not only to offer his condolences but also to tell her he would drive her free of charge whenever he could, well aware that, like many Muslim women, she did not know how to drive.

"I think everyone in Beit Hanina knows Srulik," Hoda says. "He's been coming to Ahmed and Mohammed's auto shop for forever, and even my mother-in-law knows that he gets a lot of the credit for building up their business. If he hadn't brought all of his Israeli taxi buddies, who knows what would have become of their work?"

"But Rumi is still mad at you for opening the salon?" Yasmin asks.

"Oh yes! Although I'm not sure what bothers her more—that she thinks it's not religious, or that I have a job."

She remembers how, four months after Ahmed's death, his mother Rumi was infuriated to learn of Hoda's plan to open a salon to earn some money.

"A salon?" Rumi shrieked. "Do you want the world to think we're infidels? We praise only *inner* beauty. What kind of Muslim woman goes to a salon?"

"Lots of them, actually," said Hoda. "Or at least, lots of them would go if it were easy. The law says that we have to cover our hair when we are in public, but when we are home with our husbands—or even when we look at ourselves in the mirror—why can't we look beautiful?"

Rumi just kept grumbling, but Hoda ignored her. Clearly, Rumi didn't care much about her appearance. She wore a hijab, no makeup on her leathery brown face, and shapeless, floor-length caftans of various drab colors. Hoda didn't know if Rumi dressed this poorly when her husband was alive because he had died before Ahmed and Hoda got married. But Hoda knew that it was important for a woman to feel good about herself.

Ever since she was a little girl, Hoda's mother had brought her copies of *Vogue* and other fashion magazines from Europe, and she studied these as if they were the *Qur'an*. Hoda was raised in Cairo, where her parents were in most ways traditional Muslims, but as a tailor her father flew with her mother to Paris twice a year, and the European style was a great influence on them. They were cosmopolitan, unique within their community. Hoda was proud of the way her father wore a shark-skin suit, and her mother wore long dresses of beautiful brocade. She would watch her mother carefully apply her makeup and thought she was the most beautiful woman in the world. Hoda's parents had both died within the past few years, and she misses them terribly.

"Ohhhhhhh," Hoda moans, pressing her hand to her forehead. Her head is pounding. She grips the sides of her black nylon smock, pops open the snaps running down the middle, crumples it into a ball, and tosses it into the laundry bin. Her fingers are too puffy to remove her rings before she washes up at the large sink. Afterward, she sniffs her hands. Despite wearing latex gloves all day long, the smell of peroxide permeates. It nauseates Hoda, and she tells Yasmin to open the front door.

"I can't stand this smell for another second," Hoda complains.

"It's not like it smells so much better outside—it reeks of garbage," Yasmin says, checking in the mirror to make sure her hijab has been put on properly before she opens the door. She gives Hoda a hug. "I just wish you had a husband to take care of you, especially now."

"I appreciate that," says Hoda, untangling herself from Yasmin's embrace. "But I can take care of myself. And right now, I don't have the energy for a relationship. I'm anxious about getting a kidney. And I need to focus on the boys. I'm worried about them getting into trouble, especially Khalid."

"Teenage trouble, or real trouble?" Yasmin asks, narrowing her eyes.

"Neither, I hope," says Hoda. "But he's grown a bit distant. He's out of the house more than he's in. I have no idea what he's up to."

"Well, you know how it is with teenagers. They come home for food and laundry and a place to sleep."

"Yes, it's true," says Hoda. She turns away from Yasmin and smoothes her long, black skirt. "He's becoming interested in things that I know nothing about, and it makes me feel Ahmed's absence even more."

"Like what?"

"Construction, auto repair," says Hoda. "He's started to visit the hardware store after school and luckily, they've been very nice to him, teaching him lots of stuff. I don't love the whole crowd—there are a bunch of angry men that hang around—but the owner is so generous. He gives Khalid small jobs, pays him well, and just last week even gave him a new pair of Nike sneakers."

"The hardware store?" asks Yasmin. "The one near the overpass? Hoda, you know that's just a front, right?"

"It's not just a front. They sell tools."

Yasmin snorts. "Please don't tell me you're fooled by a few shelves of hammers and nails. You know the people there are dangerous. Rumor has it they were behind that attack last year at the Tel Aviv nightclub. Keep the boys away from them."

Hoda shuts her eyes.

"If they're giving Khalid fancy sneakers, it's not because he's stocking the shelves," warns Yasmin.

"Khalid is a good boy," says Hoda, raising her voice. She squeezes her forehead and winces. "Yasmin, I have a splitting headache. Please don't lecture me."

"I'm sorry. I know Khalid is a good boy. But it worries me."

Hoda sighs and rubs her eyes. "Me, too. I'm worried about a million things, but right now my main concern is that Khalid is going to fail math. He's doing terribly, and I can't help him at all. Ahmed was the one with a head for numbers, not me."

"I'm aware of that," says Yasmin with a wry smile. "That's why I do the books."

Hoda pulls on her black, nylon ninja underscarf, a small hood attached to a neck loop that helps the scarf she uses for a hijab to stay in place. She swirls the long piece of blush chiffon once around her head, and then around her neck in the other direction, and with a final swoosh, her hijab is in place. A quick glance at her reflection in the mirror, then she picks up her bag to leave.

"I should sweep one more time, but I need a few minutes to relax before the boys get home," says Hoda.

"I just finished sweeping!" Yasmin exclaims. "I don't even know why I bother. You always do it again."

Hoda smiles. "It's my problem, not yours. Living so close to my mother-in-law has turned me into a clean freak. I'm terrified of her inspections."

"Liar. You're not scared of anybody," says Yasmin. "And besides, Rumi is more bark than bite."

"Oh, she can bark. This morning, she was screaming so loudly about the garbage strike, I could feel the windows rattling from across the courtyard."

Yasmin laughs, showing her yellowed teeth, and her stomach jiggles. "That Rumi—she's something, isn't she? Some people mellow as they age. She just seems to get angrier."

"Exactly! I want things calm and steady. She wants a roller coaster." Hoda sighs before heading to the door. "How is it that I am left without a husband but still with a mother-in-law?"

***

HODA CHECKS HER PHONE as soon as she gets out of the salon. The cell reception isn't great, and she always worries that she'll miss a call from Dr. Applebaum telling her they have a kidney for her. While she knows that he has Yasmin's phone number, as well as the phone number for the salon, it has become her habit to go outside every few hours and make sure she has no missed calls.

Obtaining a kidney transplant is even harder in Israel than in other parts of the world. A majority of both Muslims and Jews decline to donate because of the religious prohibition of desecrating the body, alive or dead. Dr. Applebaum explained this to her when she met him five years ago, when she first became sick.

It surprised Hoda that a Jewish doctor would be treating her, but she quickly realized that the hospital is its own microcosm. Doctors are doctors and patients are patients, regardless of their religion or nationality. Arab doctors treat Jewish patients, and vice versa. The focus on the universal human body helps to erase ethnic lines.

Dr. Applebaum told Hoda to ask her family members if they would consider donating a kidney. He explained to her that a person needs only one working kidney to filter waste and remove excess fluid from the body. Her sons were too young to be donors. But she was thrilled when Ahmed's younger brother Mohammed offered. Unfortunately, he turned out not to be a match.

Then Dr. Applebaum told Hoda about a kidney chain. In a kidney transplant chain, an altruistic donor—someone who has no connection to a kidney recipient—sets off a series of transplants in which family or friends of a recipient give a kidney to another person in need, essentially "trading" one kidney for another to produce better matches. Dr. Applebaum said that if Mohammed would donate his kidney first, then Hoda would be moved to the top of the transplant list. He recognized Hoda's skepticism and had an Arab colleague confirm his statement.

"I'm not sure about this, Hoda," Mohammed said. "I want to help you, but how do we know we can trust him?"

"We don't, but without this, I practically have no hope of finding a transplant in time before I need to start dialysis. And once I do, I could lose my salon, and I don't know what will happen with Khalid and Jamal."

Hoda asked Srulik to talk to Mohammed. She knew that Srulik's daughter Yael, suffering from cystic fibrosis, had undergone a double lung transplant a few years earlier. He tried to convince him, but Mohammed still resisted.

It was Mohammed's wife, Leila, who finally helped Mohammed make the decision. "It says in the *Qur'an* that a person who saves one life, it is like he saved all of mankind," she said. "Mohammed, you have an opportunity to save Hoda's life. You owe it to your late brother to help her."

Mohammed donated his kidney at the end of August, telling only his family of his plans. Rumi was infuriated. She told him she understood if he gave his kidney directly to Hoda, but it was terrible to give it to an unknown—possibly even a Jew. She refused to visit him in the hospital, but called him every day to scream at him for being a traitor and an infidel. Months later, Hoda still hasn't gotten a kidney. Twice it seemed that there would be a donor for her, but both times there was a donor health issue, and the kidney could not be transplanted.

"Burn your tongue on soup and you'll blow on yogurt,"
says Rumi, smugly reminding both her and Mohammed on a
near-daily basis that they have been tricked by the Israelis.

***

E VERY TIME HODA UNLOCKS her front door, she is grateful that her mother-in-law lives with Mohammed and his
family, instead of with her. They are in the same four-building
complex, but at least they are separated by a courtyard. When
Ahmed died in the car crash, Rumi wanted to move in to help
care for the children, but Hoda refused. Surprisingly, Rumi did
not argue. She chuckles, thinking what Ahmed would have said:
"I always knew Mohammed was her favorite son!" But Hoda
knows Rumi isn't happy living with Mohammed, either. Every
day Rumi cries over her divided hometown.

Beit Hanina, where Rumi and Hoda live, is one of the towns
that is bisected by the barrier wall into two very different neighborhoods. Here on the Israeli side, they have protected status
as "permanent residents," which entitles them to social benefits
such as healthcare and education and enables them to travel
without having to pass through military checkpoints. As ben-
eficiaries of Jerusalem municipality funds, their neighborhood
is relatively upscale, with four mosques, a community center,
and a swimming pool complex. On the other side of the wall,
however, conditions are much poorer, and residents do not have
any status.

Simply by the way the concrete was poured, Rumi's three sisters and their families ended up living on the other side of the wall. It is a constant source of distress for the proud Rumi. They tease her, because she lives in Israel, for not being an authentic Palestinian. Their family ties are also strained because they cannot see each other as often as they used to, due to the poor conditions of the roads on the other side of the wall and the lengthy wait times at the checkpoints.

Barely a day goes by when Rumi does not complain to Hoda about the Israelis. She finds a way to work the political situation into nearly every conversation.

Sure enough, just as Hoda unlocks the door to her apartment, her cell phone rings. It's Rumi.

"Hello Rumi," Hoda says. "*Keefik*? How are you today?"

"I'm terrible," grunts Rumi in her raspy voice. "And do you know why?"

"No, I don't." She sits on a kitchen chair and slides her black shoes off her sore feet.

"They tinkered with the traffic lights today on Abdul Shoman Street," Rumi says. "They made them too fast! It goes from green to red in less than thirty seconds. They want us stuck in a permanent traffic jam."

Hoda sighs. "Are you sure, Rumi? Maybe they were installing red light cameras to catch people speeding through."

"That would be even worse!" says Rumi. "We don't need to be watched by the Israelis every second like laboratory rats. They already know what we are doing and who we are talking to. For all we know, our houses are bugged!"

"Oh Rumi..." Hoda's voice trails off. "The Israelis don't have the time, the resources, or even the patience to listen to all of us." Even as she tries to reassure Rumi, she thinks about Khalid's new sneakers and feels a small knot in her stomach.

"We are traitors for living here, among Israelis," says Rumi. "We are separated from our family, our land! We should be part of the resistance, not part of the occupation!"

"*Inshallah*, we will have our own state soon," says Hoda, as patiently as possible for someone who has the same conversation every day. "But in the meantime, we are not part of the occupation, and you know that."

"If only Ahmed hadn't died in vain. If only he could have been a martyr..." Rumi laments, sobbing.

Hoda groans silently. She will ignore this dig, as she always does. How could Rumi still be angry at her son for dying in a car crash? Diabolical, she thinks. But she doesn't say a word. She feels her pulse quickening, and the doctor said she must try to keep herself relaxed. She rips open a pita and stuffs a big piece in her mouth.

A moment later, Rumi stops crying. "Are the boys home yet? I always feel better when I see my wonderful grandsons."

"Not yet, but they should be coming home soon," says Hoda.

"Should I come for dinner?" asks Rumi.

"Hmmm, I don't think so. I haven't even started cooking. You can stop by later for a minute before the boys go to the mosque for *maghrib*." Hoda doesn't wait for a reply. She hangs up the phone and sighs. She is so tired of the rhetoric. Of course, she wishes there were no soldiers, no fighting, no border wall...none of it. But what will complaining do for her? As Ahmed always said, just do honest work and stay out of trouble.

Hoda pulls her chair close to the stove and leans against it while she prepares couscous with lamb and vegetables in a tomato broth. She relishes these few moments of peace and quiet between work at the salon and work at home being a mother. Hoda stirs the food, the only noise in the room coming from the slow bubbling of the simmering pot. She inhales the smoky aroma, sprinkling in some sumac and thyme to deepen the flavor.

It seems as though she's only been home for a minute when thirteen-year-old Jamal bursts through the door. His black hair is tousled, and his cheeks are flushed. He is wearing his school knapsack and carrying a bag of onions and potatoes, which he deposits on the kitchen floor.

"Hi *Uma*! I got your stuff." Jamal gives Hoda a big hug and is startled to realize that he is now as tall as she is. Did he grow overnight? Jamal is a sweet boy, still young enough to enjoy seeing his mother at the end of the day. "Are you feeling good today?" He looks at her face searchingly.

"Hello, my boy," says Hoda with a smile. What an angel. He is so helpful, so kind. She pinches his cheek. "Yes, I'm fine. How was your day?"

"Good. How was yours?" Jamal walks into the kitchen. He spoons some couscous straight from the pot into his mouth. He smiles at Hoda. "Mmmm...this is good. I'm hungry."

"Me, too," says Hoda. "Where's your brother?"

"Khalid?" Jamal looks down at the floor.

"Of course, Khalid! Do you have another brother that I don't know about?" Hoda notices Jamal avoiding her gaze. She starts to feel the pit in her stomach returning. "Where is Khalid? Tell me now."

Jamal quickly scoops another bite of couscous into his mouth, then sits down on a kitchen chair. "Khalid said he'll be home later."

"Where did he go?"

"He stopped at the hardware store. They had a big job for him."

"A big job," murmurs Hoda. She and Jamal lock eyes. She wonders what he knows. "Did he say what time he would be home?"

"Khalid just said he would be home later. So, let's eat. I'm starving!"

Hoda sits down with Jamal, but suddenly she has no appetite. Yasmin's words are bothering her. It would be easy for those radicalized men from the hardware store to prey on eager, innocent boys like Khalid. The boys are flattered by the attention and gifts and may not realize how dangerous a task as simple as picking up a package can be.

Things would be different if Ahmed was around, she thinks, regretfully. She twists her napkin in her lap and takes a deep breath. Hoda smiles at Jamal. He tells her a funny story from school while gobbling up his dinner.

After they finish eating, Jamal leaves to go play basketball with friends. Hoda sits down in the living room and turns on the television. A picture of a charred bus carcass flashes on the screen during the Channel Two evening news. The anchor details that morning's deadly suicide bombing on Route One at the edge of Jerusalem: eight Israelis killed, many others injured in the explosion. The terrorist is identified as a Palestinian from Shuafat of East Jerusalem.

Hoda shuts off the TV and walks back into the kitchen. She vows that she will forbid Khalid from visiting the hardware store going forward. Counting the sharp knives in the drawer to make sure they're all accounted for, she says to herself as if it is a mantra: "Just do honest work and stay out of trouble."

Khalid returns home an hour later. Hoda rushes to the door.

"Khalid! Where were you?" She tries to keep the shrillness out of her voice, but she can't keep her hands from shaking.

"I was at the hardware store. I told Jamal to tell you." Khalid narrows his eyes. His black, curly hair is cropped close to his head and his thick eyebrows and thin mustache make him look much older than his fifteen years. He pecks her on the cheek. "Are you feeling okay today?"

"Yes, I am, Khalid, thank you for asking." Hoda softens. "You must be hungry. Let's get you a plate."

"I ate already." Khalid drops his knapsack off his shoulder and holds it by the top handle. "I have a ton of math to do."

"Are you understanding the algebra better?" Hoda asks. "It's really important that you do well on this next test. Your teacher said your grades have been falling."

"Yes, *Uma*," says Khalid, nodding his head. "I've been working hard at it."

"Good boy," says Hoda, smiling at him. Khalid smiles back and starts to walk past Hoda. "Wait, Khalid." She takes a deep breath. "I know you're being paid well at the hardware store, but I really don't think it's the right thing for you right now." Hoda tries to sound as nonchalant as possible. She puts her hand on Khalid's arm. "The school year will be over shortly and it's important to focus on your grades. You'll have plenty of time to find a good job in the summer."

Khalid looks at Hoda and shakes his head. "But this is a good job! *Uma*, they pay me money and they give me gifts. Haven't you noticed that I don't ask you for money anymore?"

"Yes, and I'm very proud of you for trying to help around here," says Hoda. "But I just..."

"Why don't you just say thank you?" Khalid pulls away and heads down the hallway. "I gotta go."

***

K HALID SLIPS INTO THE bedroom he shares with Jamal.
He has become adept at moving noiselessly. The bedroom is small, just wide enough for the two twin beds abutting the wall with the window and the wooden three-drawer dresser which separates them. Above Jamal's bed is a small bookshelf, and above Khalid's is a blank wall, studded with the tiny remnants of tape that had been used to hold up a martyr poster of his cousin Ismail. He was from the other side of the wall and was killed by Israeli soldiers in December after he drove his car into a crowded bus stop. Khalid did not know this cousin well, but Rumi had impressed upon him how important he was to the family.

"Ismail is a hero," she explained to Khalid the day of the funeral, when she gave him the poster depicting her nephew, cloaked in the Palestinian flag, in front of the Dome of the Rock. "He is bringing glory unto his family." She gripped Khalid's hands while she spoke, alternately stroking them and squeezing them tight. "He will be rewarded with blessings in the afterlife, and his family will receive riches in this world."

She then put her hands on Khalid's cheeks and looked him in the eye. "Dear boy, you understand? Ismail's family will never again have to worry about money. His family will be paid handsomely for his sacrifice."

Khalid wriggled out of Rumi's grasp.

"There are different levels of *shahid*, you know, my sweet boy," murmured Rumi reassuringly. "Not only like Ismail. Being a lookout, being a courier...there are many ways to help."

She helped Khalid hang the poster on his wall while Hoda was at work. Later that night, when Hoda discovered it, she was furious. She yanked it off and ripped it into small pieces.

"Ismail was a powerless kid who was used as a pawn, and now he's dead," fumed Hoda. "There's nothing to idolize here."

Khalid sits on his bed and takes out a shrink-wrapped Apple box from his knapsack. He removes the small, black envelope taped to the bottom and stuffs it in his pocket. Then he unwraps his new iPhone and taps on the glass. Just as he is uploading TikTok, Jamal enters the bedroom.

Jamal jumps onto Khalid's bed. "Where'd you get that?"

"None of your business." Khalid shoves Jamal out of the way and quickly puts the phone back into his bag.

"You got that from those men in the hardware store, didn't you?" Jamal tries to grab the phone from Khalid.

"I told you—it's none of your business! Get off!" Khalid pushes Jamal, who falls onto the floor.

"You must be selling a lot of tools. First chocolates, then sneakers, now a new phone?" Jamal jumps back onto Khalid's bed.

"Stop annoying me!" Khalid puts on his headphones and takes out his math book and a pencil from his knapsack. "I need to do my homework. Leave me alone."

"I want a new phone," Jamal says, bouncing back onto Khalid's bed. "How about getting me a job?"

Khalid sighs, removes his headphones, and gives Jamal a weary look. "Trust me, it's nothing you want to do. The next time they give me a gift, I'll give it to you. But only if you swear in the name of *Allah* that you will not tell *Uma* about this."

"Don't be stupid, Khalid," says Jamal, looking serious now.

Khalid doesn't answer. He scratches something in his notebook.

"I've seen the police there," Jamal insists.

Khalid cracks his knuckles a few times but says nothing.

"You know *Uma* hasn't been feeling well lately," Jamal continues. "She's so tired all the time. Don't make her worse."

"You idiot! I'm trying to help her!" Khalid throws his pencil down and scowls at Jamal. "I'm the only one here who isn't a money drain on her all the time. Now leave me alone and don't say anything or else you'll be sorry."

***

WHILE THE BOYS ARE in their room, Hoda calls Mohammed's wife Leila, her sister-in-law and close friend. Leila and Mohammed have two girls, Amal and Aisha, who are just a bit older than Hoda's boys. When Ahmed died, Mohammed began coming to Hoda's house every morning to take Khalid and Jamal to pray with him at the mosque before school. Hoda wished he would be more of a father figure to the boys, playing cards and football with them and helping them study, but he would not spend time in their home, reminding her of the Prophet's admonition: "*Beware upon entering of women...[even] the brother-in-law is death.*" Leila has been a constant source of support, though, filling in at the salon when Yasmin is out. She is the closest family Hoda has nearby.

"Hello, Leila?" Hoda says.

"Hoda, hi! How are you feeling?" Leila asks.

"I'm fine, just fine. Uh, I'm sure I'm overreacting in some way..." Hoda starts.

"As you usually do, sister!" Leila interrupts, laughing.

"Yes, yes," says Hoda, laughing herself. "But seriously..." she whispers. "Khalid has been spending a lot of time at the hardware store lately. I know Mohammed helped get him a job there, and I'm very grateful, but I think maybe he should just focus on his schoolwork for now."

"Really? Mohammed says he is doing great at the store," Leila replies. "Isn't it helpful to have some extra money coming in?"

"I just don't think it's a good idea. I want him to stop."

"Okay, I will speak to him. But Rumi will be the harder person to convince."

Hoda's throat feels dry. "Rumi? What does she have to do with the hardware store?"

Leila waits a moment before replying. "It was Rumi's idea in the first place that Khalid should work there. And with Ahmed gone, Mohammed also feels a certain responsibility for Khalid and Jamal."

"To teach them violence? To put them in harm's way?" asks Hoda. The knot in Hoda's stomach is getting bigger, and she regrets calling Leila.

"Of course not!" says Leila. "Mohammed is your family! You've got to trust him, okay? You may not see eye-to-eye with him on everything, but he's a good person. In the name of *Allah*, he gave his kidney for you!"

"Of course, I know, I'm sorry. You know I appreciate it more than anything." Hoda's head is spinning. She squeezes the bridge of her nose with her fingers. "Forget I said anything. I think it's just this new medication I'm on. It's making me crazy."

"I hope you feel good, Hoda. Have a good night."

***

Later in the evening, Hoda is washing her floor, the brown stone darkening with each swipe of the mop, when she hears a knock at the door. She peeks through the eyehole and groans: Rumi.

Barely five feet tall, Rumi wears a hijab and a flowy, floor-length djellaba in a chestnut brown color. Her mouth is twisted into a permanent scowl, but she is not completely unattractive; her cheekbones remain high and prominent.

"Hello Rumi, let me tell the boys you are here," says Hoda, putting the mop aside. "Watch out, the floor is still wet."

"Yes, and there's still some dirt over there," says Rumi, pointing with her finger to the corner of the room.

"Ah, yes," nods Hoda, turning her face towards the corner so that Rumi will not see her rolling her eyes. "Thank you for pointing that out."

Rumi doesn't seem to notice the sarcastic drip in Hoda's voice. "Anytime, dear."

Hoda motions for Rumi to sit on the couch in the living area while she gets the boys.

"Wait, before you get the boys—are you feeling all right?"

Hoda is shocked. Rumi rarely asks her anything about herself. "I'm fine, why do you ask?"

"You don't look very good. Your ankles are swollen like watermelons, and you look very tired." Rumi says. "Any news on a kidney?"

"No Rumi," says Hoda, grimacing. "No news."

"Ah, I thought not," says Rumi.

Khalid and Jamal come out of their room and greet Rumi with a peck on each cheek.

"My boys!" Rumi wraps her arms around them, forcing them to sit alongside her in crouching positions. "How is school going? Everything good?"

"Yes, *Sitto*," the boys answer in unison. Khalid is the first to squirm out of Rumi's tight embrace. Once he breaks loose, Jamal follows. They stand awkwardly by the couch.

"Anything new?" Rumi looks back and forth between the boys.

"I scored two goals in my football game yesterday," says Jamal.

"Excellent!" says Rumi, clapping her hands. "And Khalid, Mohammed told me you've been working at the hardware store. That's wonderful!"

Hoda is in the kitchen, pretending to mop, and her ears perk up.

"They are not having you work too hard, are they?" Rumi asks in a gentle voice.

"No, it's fine," Khalid answers.

Hoda feels her heart pounding. "Rumi, I think Khalid should be focusing on his schoolwork," she says, still holding the mop while walking towards the couch.

Rumi gives Hoda a steely look. "I think it's good for a boy like Khalid to have a job."

Hoda tilts her head questioningly. "Even if that job might be too much for a fifteen-year-old to handle?"

"*Uma*, it's not too much for me," interjects Khalid.

Rumi maintains her gaze. "He is a good boy, just like his father." She stands up and ushers the boys toward the door.

"If Ahmed were alive, he would want Khalid to focus on school," insists Hoda.

Rumi ignores her. "Come, boys, I'll walk out with you. Mohammed will be waiting outside to go with you to the mosque."

Hoda blocks the door with her mop. "No. The boys will pray at home tonight."

Khalid and Jamal look up, surprised. "Why?" asks Jamal.

"I need you home tonight. I don't feel great, and you both have a lot of homework."

"I thought you just said you were fine," asks Rumi, squinting at her. "Should I get a doctor?"

"No."

"Then the boys should go to the mosque."

"Rumi, it is not forbidden to pray at home," says Hoda, shaking the mop at Rumi. "It is perfectly fine to pray anywhere as long as the floor is clean. Do you see how often I am washing the floor?"

"Maybe it is not forbidden, but it is *Mustahab* to pray in a mosque," says Rumi. "*Allah* answers the prayers of those in a congregation twenty-five times more than just one person's."

Hoda doesn't move from the door. She rarely stands up to Rumi. Without any family of her own, she needs Rumi's support. But the control Rumi exerts over her and the boys is becoming intolerable.

"The boys are just a few blocks from the mosque," Rumi says. "And they can hear *Adhan*. How can they ignore the call to prayer?"

"I'll go, and Jamal can stay with *Uma*," says Khalid, looking at Rumi. She gives him an approving smile.

"No, both of you are staying home," says Hoda firmly. "You can pray and then you need to finish your homework."

Khalid looks back and forth from his mother to his grandmother, then he shifts his gaze to the floor.

Rumi doesn't try to hide her displeasure. She sneers, "If my son were here, you can be sure these boys would be at the mosque five times a day."

"If your son were here, a lot of things would be different," says Hoda. "Goodnight, Rumi." Hoda opens the front door and practically pushes Rumi out.

A few minutes later, she watches Jamal and Khalid do the *wudu*, or ritual ablution, in preparation for the *Isha* prayer. They wash their arms, hands, face, and feet. They face the back wall of the living room, which is the direction of Mecca in Saudi Arabia.

Khalid turns around and sees Hoda standing in the doorway. He looks at her with a confused expression and asks, "Do you want to pray with us?"

Hoda shakes her head, no. "I'm going to bed."

***

IN HER BEDROOM, HODA flops down on the bed. It's only nine o'clock, but she's exhausted. She's only been dozing for a short while when her cell phone rings. Hoda answers sleepily, assuming it's Rumi.

"Rumi, I just can't talk anymore tonight. I am so unbelievably tired."

"Ahem, Mrs. Ibrahim, this is Dr. Applebaum on the phone."

"Oh, my goodness, I'm sorry!" Hoda bolts upright in bed. "Dr. Applebaum, is it—do you have a kidney for me?"

"Yes! Yes I do, Hoda, and I pray this time it works," he says. "It's a cadaver kidney, but a near-perfect match. You need to be at Hadassah Ein-Kerem as soon as you can for pre-op, and we will perform the transplant a short while after. You'll need to enter through the emergency department since it's so late, and we'll get you from there."

"Praised be *Allah*! Oh, thank you, Dr. Applebaum!"

"I'm sorry you had to wait so long, Hoda," says Dr. Applebaum. "Let's hope the third time's a charm."

"Thank you, doctor. I'll see you soon."

Hoda has been waiting for this day for nearly eight months. Just as when she had been preparing for childbirth, she has a packed hospital bag sitting in her closet. She quickly calls Leila and tells her the good news. Before Hoda has a chance to ask, Leila says Mohammed will pick her up within the hour to take her to the hospital.

Hoda runs into the boys' room. They are both sitting on their beds, still doing schoolwork.

"Khalid, Jamal!"

"What is it, *Uma*?" Jamal jumps up. He looks stricken with worry.

"Dr. Applebaum just called. They have a kidney for me! *Alhamdulillah*, I am getting a kidney!" Hoda is clasping her hands to her chest and smiling widely.

"You are? You're going to be cured?" Jamal gives Hoda a big hug.

Khalid looks up at Hoda. "Where did they get the kidney from?"

Hoda looks at him. "From a dead person. I don't know anything about him...or her. But it doesn't matter—Dr. Applebaum said it's a perfect match."

"So, you don't know who it's from?"

"No, I don't. Khalid, why does this matter?"

"What if it's from a Jew?" Khalid practically spits the words out.

"What if?" Hoda isn't smiling anymore. "I don't care if it's from an alien from outer space as long as it cures me."

"I couldn't live with myself if I had a piece of Jew in me," says Khalid.

"Well, then, I guess it's good that I'm the one getting the kidney. We're leaving here soon. Mohammed will drive us. Make sure you're ready."

"Tonight?" Khalid sputters. "I was supposed to study with a friend later."

Hoda squints at him. "This late at night?"

Khalid meets her gaze. "Well, we both had a lot to do earlier, and we are good study partners."

Hoda nods. "So, you'll study on the phone from the hospital." She inhales deeply. "I need to be as calm and relaxed as possible going into this surgery. I need you boys with me at the hospital. I don't want to have to worry about you."

***

A SHORT WHILE LATER, Mohammed drives Hoda, Jamal, and Khalid to the hospital. They spend the ride in sleepy silence. Once they get there, Mohammed offers to come in with Hoda and stay with the boys.

"Thanks Mohammed, that's really nice of you." Hoda is surprised at Mohammed's generosity. "But it's so late! You don't want to go to sleep?"

"Not a bother at all. I've been waiting for this day to come." Mohammed smiles. His olive face reddens. "*Inshallah*, soon you will be in good health."

Hoda feels tears welling up in her eyes. "Mohammed, thank you. I...I don't know what else to say. I would not be here today if it were not for you."

"It is *Allah's* wish. Let's go."

Inside the waiting room of the emergency department, there is a cacophony of Arabic, Hebrew, and English mingled in conversation. It's crowded, especially considering the late hour. Among the people waiting are a Haredi Jewish man and his heavily pregnant wife, sitting huddled together in the corner, mumbling into their prayer books. Two elderly, hijab-wearing Arab women are chatting animatedly. A priest dressed in a long brown robe paces back and forth along the back wall. A red-haired, young Israeli soldier sits quietly by himself, with his head in his hands. He is not in uniform, but has an imposing gun sticking up from behind his shoulder.

A nurse shows Hoda where to go for pre-op testing. "Your husband can come with you, but your children will have to wait here."

"Oh no...he's not my husband," says Hoda.

"Well, then, he needs to stay here, too," says the nurse.

Hoda frowns. This was not part of her plan. "*Alhamdulillah* that you came with me," she says to Mohammed. "I would hate for the boys to wait here alone."

Mohammed sits down on a chair, folding his long legs, and gestures to the couch next to him. "They'll be right here with me, and they'll be fine, Hoda. Don't worry about anything. Go, and if we can wait with you when you are done with the testing, call me."

Hoda takes a deep breath. "Yes, okay, thank you so much." She puts one hand on each boy's face. "Khalid, Jamal. Listen to Mohammed. I'll see you very soon."

"Bye, *Uma*," says Jamal, hugging her tightly.

"Bye," says Khalid, kissing her on the cheek.

"Goodbye my loves," says Hoda, blinking back tears. "I love you."

Hoda goes through the glass double doors into a long corridor, and she is gone. Jamal sits down next to Mohammed, but Khalid remains standing.

"Aren't you going to sit down, Khalid?" asks Mohammed.

Khalid shifts his weight from one foot to the other. He palms the phone in his pocket and feels to make sure the small black envelope is still taped securely to its back. "I, uh, I need to make a delivery."

Mohammed squints at Khalid. "A delivery?"

"For, uh, the hardware store," says Khalid. "I didn't know *Uma* would be in the hospital. I promised them I would deliver something tonight."

"Go along then," says Mohammed, stroking his thick, black beard. "Your mother will be a long time anyway. If she finishes early, I'll tell her you went to get something to eat."

"Thank you." Khalid turns to leave.

"Aren't you taking Jamal?"

"What?" Khalid wheels around, his face reddening. "No, I don't think...I mean, what will he do?"

"I don't want to leave *Uma*," protests Jamal.

Mohammed beckons Khalid with his finger to come closer. He pats the couch next to him and tells Khalid to sit down. He leans in close to Jamal and Khalid and speaks to them in a whisper: "Your mother has a long recovery ahead of her. Don't you think you need to do everything you can to help her? Khalid—Jamal is old enough to have a job, too. Take him with you so he can see how it's done, and I will speak to the men about getting both of you a reward."

Khalid squirms in his seat. Jamal looks ready to cry.

"No! I will get a job if you want me to, but not now," pleads Jamal. "I don't want to leave *Uma*."

"Your mother will be absolutely fine," says Mohammed, re-assuringly, looking Jamal in the eye. "You'll be back well before the surgery. The testing itself takes hours."

"I don't think it's a good idea to take Jamal," argues Khalid. "I don't need a crybaby with me."

"I'm not a crybaby!" splutters Jamal.

"Enough!" says Mohammed, his dark eyes flashing. "I'm done arguing. Go!"

Khalid jumps up and walks quickly towards the door. Jamal trips over his feet, trying to catch up with him.

"Don't be so clumsy all the time!" Khalid admonishes him. "We have to be quick."

They exit the hospital and walk about two blocks north, alongside a wide, four-lane boulevard. The bright street lights illuminate the sidewalk. There is a crowded bus stop at the corner. Four male soldiers stand there, in uniform, their large, black Tavor rifles strapped across their chests. They're checking people's identification documents and looking at their faces—usual protocol after a bus bombing. As the boys near the intersection, the soldiers turn and face them.

The soldiers are only a few years older than Khalid, but in their uniforms and with their guns, they look intimidating. Three of them are tall, close to six feet each, with broad shoulders and bulky arm muscles that strain the sleeves of their olive-green shirts. The fourth soldier—a short, slight boy—has a stubbornness to his chiseled jaw. Their guns glow under the bright streetlight.

Khalid feels the hand holding onto the phone in his pocket turn clammy. Beads of sweat appear on his forehead. "Let's turn around," he says to Jamal. "We can go later."

"After all that? He'll kill us if we come back now," says Jamal. "Let's go."

"No, Jamal, I think those soldiers are going to mess with us." Khalid keeps fingering the phone and the envelope in his pocket.

"Why? We've done nothing wrong, and we have our IDs," insists Jamal. "Didn't you say you have to make a delivery tonight? It's so late already! Let's just go!"

Jamal keeps walking up the street. Khalid's heart starts beating fast. He stops walking, but Jamal keeps going. "Jamal!" he whisper-shouts. "Jamal!"

Jamal turns around. "Khalid! Come on, I thought you said we had to hurry—let's go!"

Two of the taller soldiers walk towards the boys.

"Cross the street, now!" Khalid barks at Jamal.

Jamal runs into the road without looking. A car swerves and nearly hits him.

"Hey kids, watch out!" The two approaching soldiers yell in rudimentary Arabic from the curb. "Where are you rushing to?"

Through clenched teeth, Khalid tells Jamal to keep walking. He keeps a firm grip on the phone in his pants.

"Hey kids! Hold up one second." The soldiers start to cross the street in a slow jog.

"Run!" Khalid shouts. The boys veer right, away from the intersection, to a part of the street that is being repaired. Three orange traffic cones dot the rocky pavement. Chunks of tar are everywhere.

"Stop!" the soldiers shout. "Stop!"

Another soldier is on the other side of the street. He's off-duty, not in uniform, but still wearing a gun slung over his shoulder. He is tall and thin, red-haired, with a freckled face. He's looking down at the ground as he weaves along the sidewalk, muttering to himself. When the other soldiers start shouting, his head snaps up. Khalid and Jamal are just a few hundred feet ahead of him.

"I've got them!" he shouts to the soldiers. To the boys he screams: "Stop!"

Khalid and Jamal keep running.

The red-headed soldier runs after them. "Stop!"

Khalid doesn't stop. Jamal keeps running, too, but just then, he stumbles on a rock, losing his footing.

At the same moment, the red-headed soldier stops, shoulders his rifle, flicks the safety, aims low, and shoots.

Liver

ONCE AGAIN, DAVID SASSOON stands amid a pile of fresh dates, their yellow flesh punctured by his mother's bite marks. Sometimes the heap is so high, he struggles to see his mother. But he can hear her complaining bitterly that she misses her old life in Iraq. David tries to console her, and he calls out: "Mama!"

"David, David!" Rachel Sassoon shakes his shoulder. "Wake up!"

David's eyes flutter open. He's surprised to see it's already dark outside. He tries to sit up, but he's been lying on the recliner in the living room all Saturday and can't summon the energy. Despite the warm April weather, he huddles under a blanket.

"You were crying for your mother."

"They say if you keep dreaming about your dead parents, it's because they're waiting for you at heaven's gates," whispers David. "I'm going to die soon."

Rachel sighs as she plucks a towel to fold from the pile of laundry on the couch. "No one has any idea what dreams mean, and besides, what makes you think you're going to heaven?"

David half-smiles, but he feels the gut punch. There it is—the denigration of the day. Not that she isn't justified. He hasn't been a very good husband these past few years, as his liver disease has worsened and he has become little more than a lump on a couch. He tries not to look in the mirror much anymore, but he knows he looks very different from the dark, rugged, fit man he once was. If only people who marry young could always hold that younger image of each in their minds, regardless of their real age. He watches Rachel sorting the laundry across the room. She's not the same glowing, auburn-haired beauty she was at nineteen. The deep worry lines on her forehead are pronounced no matter what her facial expression, and her jowls seem pulled into permanent frowns. His illness is taking a toll on her health, too.

David has been suffering from primary sclerosing cholangitis, a chronic liver disease, for the past twelve years. Just as his doctors predicted, his liver finally weakened to the point that it is barely functioning, and he needs a transplant. No one in the family is a match, and although David is high on the organ waiting list, nothing has materialized. His doctors are beginning to despair that if he doesn't get the transplant soon, he will be too sick to be helped. The jaundice has made his skin and eyes yellow; the swelling in his legs and abdomen make him look bloated; the buildup of toxins in his blood makes it difficult to concentrate. He's nauseous and itchy and overall miserable.

"What are you staring at?"

David shakes his head and closes his eyes. "Nothing."

Rachel sighs again as she gets up from the couch. The frayed brown cushion stays sunken from where she was sitting. She pounds it with her fists to plump it up, then picks up the stack of folded towels and carries them out of the room.

David feels a burning sense of shame about burdening his family. He's embarrassed to think about how he must look, just lying around waiting for the liver transplant that will likely never happen.

No wonder he dreams about his childhood. For as hard as the past was, the present is far more painful. David was born into squalor in a *ma'abara* (transit camp) in the middle of Israel, in a town now called Or Yehuda. His parents came from Iraq in 1952 with more than one hundred thousand other Iraqi Jews in a mass emigration called Operation Ezra and Nehemiah. Although Jews had lived in harmony with their Arab neighbors in Iraq for centuries, they were forced out by rising anti-Semitism that started with the rise of Nazism in Germany and culminated with the creation of the State of Israel in 1948, when practicing Judaism became illegal in Iraq.

His family had been wealthy, working as textile traders and living in a three-story villa just a few blocks from the king's palace in Baghdad. But they came to Israel as paupers. Before they left Iraq, they had to relinquish all assets in addition to renouncing their citizenship.

His mother always said losing their motherland had been one of the most painful parts of leaving.

"We belong in Iraq! We were there for two thousand years—we built the country," she would cry. "To think we can never go back...never see our homes, never swim in the Tigris, never eat another perfect date."

David's parents joined many other Mizrahi Jews who were exiled from Arab countries, such as Iraq, Morocco, Yemen, and Algeria. Living conditions in the *ma'abara* were poor. It was composed of tin shacks, a kindergarten, a school, a grocery store, and a health clinic. There was limited water and electricity, poor sanitation, and overcrowding. As a newly established country, Israel did not have the capability or resources to care for so many new immigrants, and there already was an influx of Holocaust survivors emigrating from Europe.

Three years into their five-year stay in the *ma'abara*, David was born, and one year later, his father died of a stroke. He has only one picture of his father, taken at a wedding before they left Iraq. His bushy black mustache stands out against his white suit.

"You're thinking about your father now?" Rachel asks.

"What?" David is startled out of his reverie.

"You're pulling at your mustache. Whenever you're thinking about your father, you do that."

David shrugs.

"Well, I don't have the luxury of sentimental thinking right now, because *Pesach* is around the corner and we have lots to do," says Rachel. "You won't be any help this year."

David winces. The second denigration of the day.

"I'm going to have to interrupt those lovebirds out there," Rachel says, looking towards the sliding glass door to the balcony.

In the dark of the moonless evening, he can see only the entwined silhouettes of their son, Ezra, and his girlfriend, Leeron Levy. They've been together since the first year of high school, where they both sang for the choir. The couple has only a few more hours together before they must return to their respective bases of the Israel Defense Forces. Now, they stand pressed together by the railing overlooking Nissim Bachar Street, kissing while caressing each other.

David blushes and turns away. It's a tough juxtaposition, seeing the kids go at it when he and Rachel haven't had sex in months. Would that illness were the only reason, he rues. The truth is, their marriage has been rocky for a while, and it is only the shared hustle and bustle of life with the kids and the restaurant that's helped camouflage it. Now that all the work falls on Rachel, the tension between them is palpable.

"I feel bad to bother them," says Rachel. "It's amazing how different Ezra is when she's around. Leeron is such a calming presence for him."

"It's like she pops this balloon of anger, and all of his tension just fizzles out," says David. "She looks tough—especially in her uniform—but she's such a sweetheart."

Rachel gently raps on the glass door to the balcony. Ezra and Leeron keep kissing. She knocks again, harder, then slides open the door.

"Hey!" Rachel clears her throat. "Ezra!"

"*Ema!*" Ezra jumps away from Leeron and pulls down his white t-shirt. His freckled face reddens. "I'm sorry."

"It's okay, *motek*," Rachel says with a weary half-smile. "I was young once." She turns and picks up the small, stainless-steel wine press from the corner of the small balcony. "But now is not time for fun. *Pesach* is almost here, and we need to make the *halek* already."

David waits for Ezra to acknowledge him. Lately, he feels invisible. As if his body truly is just another lump on the couch. It's hard for him to feel like he matters to anyone anymore. He doesn't think Rachel meant to shame him about not being able to help, but maybe she did. The past year has been hard on her, but it's been even harder on him. And the *halek* is David's family's tradition.

Halek is a date paste that Iraqi Jews eat at *Pesach* (Passover), the holiday that celebrates the freedom of the Jewish people from Egyptian slavery. Its thick, sticky consistency is supposed to resemble the mortar of the bricks that Jews were forced to use thousands of years ago. Even though David never lived in Iraq, his mother painted such a vivid picture that he felt as if he had. She told him stories about the vendors who came on camels to their house to sell their wares; about swimming in the Tigris river, with water so clear you could see all the fish; and about her villa's beautiful courtyard, with pomegranate, lemon, and apricot trees, and her favorite, stately date palms. And of course, she taught him how to cook all of the Iraqi delicacies.

Years of watching his mother prepare the *kubbeh*, *ungriyi*, *mhasha*, and other traditional dishes were better than any culinary school. David knows how to wrangle his finger into the cooked semolina flour dumplings to make the perfect indentation for the meat stuffing. His stuffed eggplant with cinnamon-spiced lamb and pine nuts expertly combines sweet and sour tastes. His tangy soups have just the right amount of citrus.

Rachel, a fourth-generation Jerusalemite, eventually acquired a taste for Iraqi food after many years of marriage. David suspected her initial resistance was out of loyalty to her parents, who were furious that she was marrying an "Arab Jew," as they called him, because of his Mizrahi origins. Despite having been born and raised in Israel and having served in the army like any other Israeli, there remained a widespread discrimination towards those who came from Arab countries. Their dark skin and Arabic language made them second-class citizens.

David remained loyal to his culinary roots. He saw there were many immigrants like him who craved the Iraqi cuisine, as it brought back wonderful memories. A few years into their marriage, with David's fortieth birthday looming—and both of them deeply unhappy as they struggled with infertility—Rachel finally gave in, agreeing to let David quit his job as an electronics salesman so that he could open a small restaurant called *Taim* (tasty) in the Iraqi section of Machane Yehuda, Jerusalem's largest open market.

Within a few short months of the restaurant's opening, Rachel finally became pregnant with their first child, Ezra. That had been more than twenty years ago. David felt the dichotomy intensely: Ezra had grown up in a flash; they had slaved at the restaurant for an eternity.

Rachel stands on the balcony with her hands on her hips. "*Shabbat* is over, and I need to open the restaurant. I won't be back until after midnight, so let's get to work," she says. "Are you sure you remember how to use this wine press? It's simple, but messy. You..."

"*Ema*, I know how to use it," says Ezra, interrupting Rachel while sliding his arms through hers, forcing her into a hug. "Leeron and I will take care of it right now, don't worry. By the time you come back from the restaurant, there will be a big pot of date juice waiting for you."

"And the balcony will be all cleaned up."

"All cleaned up," echoes Leeron. Her cheeks are flushed and she has pulled her long, brown hair back into a low ponytail. "I'm happy to help, too."

Rachel smiles gratefully at Leeron.

"Is *Abba* sleeping?" asks Ezra.

"I'm not sleeping, just resting," says David, hoping his voice doesn't reveal his heavy lethargy. "And I can help with the *halek*, just maybe not the press. I can mix in the nuts."

"That will be perfect, because I have to leave in a little while," says Leeron. "Maybe Ayelet and Shachar can help, too?"

"The twins are having a sleepover at Merav's house for her birthday," says Rachel. "Nine thirteen-year-old girls in one tiny room...good luck to her parents."

"I barely got to see them this weekend," says Ezra. "Do they even miss me while I'm away?"

"Of course they do, but they had a birthday party," says Rachel, clapping her hands. "Now, let's get down to business."

Until this year, Rachel and David made the *halek* on their own. It's an arduous process, even with pre-pitted dates. They use ten kilos of dried dates to make about six liters of *halek*—enough for the whole family to enjoy for the week-long *Pesach* holiday. First, they soak the dates overnight in a pot of boiling water. Then they put them into the mesh bag of the wine press and rotate the handle of the press to squeeze out as much juice as possible. This is the hardest part—requiring a lot of arm strength—and also the messiest part, as the date juice often splatters everywhere. Finally, once all the dates are squeezed dry, they boil the date juice for about eight hours until it becomes thick and syrupy like molasses. Rachel and David always did the work outside on the balcony so they could hose it down afterward.

David smiles as he remembers how he and Rachel used to put on their bathing suits to make the *halek* because they would inevitably get dirty from the dates and soaked from the water. They were so playful then, but now...David feels a knot in his chest. They never have fun.

"Are you sure you can still add in the nuts?" Rachel asks, suddenly tender. She covers David with the knitted green wool afghan from the couch and kisses his forehead.

Sensing only pitiful condescension, David growls: "*Betach*! What do you think I am—an invalid?"

After the date juice cools, it gets mixed with ground almonds and ground walnuts. David never needs any measurements—he knows just by eyeballing it how much will be necessary. Eating *halek* since infancy, he knows the ideal consistency. It's why he never lets anyone else add in the nuts; but today, David fears he won't even have the strength for this simple task. He's grateful Ezra and Leeron have offered to help. Rachel has too much work, taking care of the house and the restaurant. This day of rest went by too quickly, as it does every Saturday.

Although Rachel and David are not strictly observant Jews, their restaurant is closed on *Shabbat* because of its location. Machane Yehuda is an open-air market in the middle of Jerusalem that dates back to the nineteenth century. Also known as the *shuk*, the market spans a fairly large section of streets and a wide selection of goods. Every type of food is sold here, including fresh fish, meat, cheese, eggs, baked goods, fruits, vegetables, candies, coffee, tea, spices, and nuts. Gourmet, artisanal, farm-fresh, organic—everything. There also are stalls selling flowers, housewares, clothing, even art. Many neighboring shops seem to offer the same things, but long-time customers know at which one to buy the eggplants and at which the lemons.

In recent years, with the gentrification of the market to include small bars, restaurants, and even music clubs, the *shuk* reopens on Saturday nights for its nightlife. The neighborhood is full of students, and the party scene is lively, with the scent of marijuana heavy in the air. There is usually just one hour of quiet on Saturday nights between four a.m. when the bars close, and five a.m. when the stalls open on Sunday.

. "Go, Rachel," David struggles to sit up straight in the recliner. "Ezra, Leeron, and I will handle things here. Manya is probably at the restaurant already, waiting for you."

Rachel gives a half-smile. "It's a good thing we live so close to the *shuk*."

David laughs softly, watching Rachel shut the door behind her. It's a long-running joke between the two of them. He thought he was brilliant, buying an apartment in the hipster Nachlaot neighborhood of Jerusalem, at the edge of Agrippas Street, where the *shuk* begins. But Rachel complained endlessly about the noise, the crowding, and the smells. Only now that she is older does she admit to David how much she appreciates her one-block commute.

Ezra squats down on the floor next to the recliner. "It's good to see you laughing, *Abba*," he says. His cropped red hair shines from the overhead light, and his freckles have darkened from the flush of his passion. "I've been worried about you."

"Don't worry about nothing except that we better get this done before *Ema* gets back, or we're all in trouble."

"We'll get it done, don't worry." Ezra adjusts the blanket around David. "It's rare that the girls are out and it's so quiet. Let's talk for a minute while Leeron is in the bathroom."

Shabbat is the only day it's quiet in Nachlaot. Normally, the neighborhood throbs with underground drilling and other head-pounding sounds of construction. But there is no construction on *Shabbat*, and the restaurants and bars are just starting to open up for the night.

David looks expectantly at Ezra. "*Nu*? What is it?"

"Nothing...we just don't talk so much anymore," says Ezra. "I miss our conversations."

"Well, I lie here like a corpse all day, so I have nothing to say." David hears the bitterness in his voice and is surprised at himself for revealing it to Ezra.

"*Abba*, you're not dead! You're going to get better."

David and Ezra lock eyes, and then both look away.

"I think we both know that's not true," David says quietly.

Ezra bites his lip as his face pales. "Why don't you rest while we do the press?"

David nods. He feels himself slumping in his chair. His eyes are heavy. He allows himself to doze.

In his dream, he remembers when Ezra was born. He can't picture his newborn face, but he can recall a feeling of happiness unlike anything else he ever experienced. After their years of infertility, Ezra was a miracle. His mother was thrilled to have a boy who could be named after David's father, and Rachel's parents were relieved that their grandson's looks belied his Mizrahi ancestry: he was pale-skinned, with a shock of bright red hair. For the first time since they got married, David felt accepted by

Rachel's parents. With this good memory on his mind, David sinks into a deep slumber.

Outside on the balcony, Ezra and Leeron work the press for a while, squeezing the dates into a big pot of liquid. While she is spraying water to clean the sticky mess on the tiled floor, Leeron takes the hose like a machine gun and playfully turns it on Ezra. He whoops, then grabs the hose from her and aims it in a steady stream at her body, soaking her t-shirt and jeans until they are dripping wet. Occasionally, he raises the nozzle so the water will splash her face, but when he does this, he partially covers the opening with his fingers so that the force won't hurt her cheeks.

"*Dai*! Stop!" Leeron is laughing so hard her chest heaves, and she's practically gasping. "My stomach hurts from laughing so much." She collapses onto the wicker loveseat. Leeron leans back and closes her eyes, catching her breath and stretching her legs out in front of her.

Ezra drops the hose and turns off the water. He sits down next to Leeron and gently strokes her hair. "The accident took a lot out of you."

"I can't think about it anymore."

Leeron is in the second year of her mandatory army service, working as a shooting instructor for an infantry unit based near Tel Aviv. Her job is a common one for women, despite the Israeli army's allowance for females to serve in combat units. A woman's stereotypical patience and intuition make her an ideal teacher for such a dangerous subject.

Two weeks ago, Leeron was in charge of a group of nineteen-
and twenty-year-olds who had just enlisted with the military
police and were less than a month into their basic training. That
fateful morning, Leeron had them assemble at the firing range
to practice using their M-16 rifles. They gathered on the large
cement slab facing the field of sand, rocks, and used bullet shells,
with body-shaped targets hanging on sticks fifty meters away.
Leeron stood with one foot on top of the big metal container of
copper bullets while she reminded them of the safety protocols,
as she did every time she led a group at the firing range.

"Always keep your gun facing forward and pointing sky-
ward."

"Don't insert a magazine or chamber a bullet until I tell you."

"Keep the safety on until I tell you."

"When you release the safety, check and check again that it is
set to semi-automatic, *not* automatic."

"Finger away from the trigger until I tell you it is time to
shoot."

"The weapon may have a safe mode, but it does not have a
brain. It is a stupid instrument and has no way of knowing what
mode it's on, or for that matter, who it's aimed at. It relies on
you. Don't be stupid."

Leeron repeated these safety instructions throughout the
day, never omitting even one word. That morning, as usual,
Leeron had her cadets practice shooting in three positions: lying
down, kneeling, and standing. In between changing positions,
she checked every weapon to make sure it was unloaded; she did

this both by giving it a visual check and by sticking a finger into the chamber. She reminded them to lay their guns in the indent between the shoulder and the chest, in just the place you would burp a baby, to best absorb the recoil.

Leeron put on her bulky headphones. The soldiers put in their foam earplugs.

Despite the warnings, one of the cadets mistakenly set her rifle to automatic and was so stunned by the fierce recoil when she fired that she could not control her weapon. It spun out of control and shot a neighboring cadet multiple times in the legs. Fortunately, the wounded cadet survived, but to Leeron the accident was as devastating as if she had died.

Leeron was immediately summoned for an investigation but was released without suspension when all the cadets in attendance vouched for her clear instructions upon their entry to the firing range. No one understood why the cadet would set her rifle to automatic against orders, or why she released her safety catch. The cadet remained under the care of a military psychiatrist and would likely not return to service.

"I'm sorry I couldn't be there for you," Ezra whispers. "My commander wouldn't grant me leave, no matter how many times I asked."

"I know," Leeron says. She squeezes his hand. "I'm not upset with you. I've got half a mind to remove the firing pin from the M-16 of the next cadet that looks stupid. Idiot will have to dry hump from now on, the *ben zona*."

Leeron stands up and leans over the railing of the second-floor balcony. The Sassoon's building, like many others in the neighborhood, is tall and thin with awkward angles, so the balcony juts out partway over another balcony below. The street below is narrow, with barely room for two cars to pass. All the streets in Nachlaot are packed with cars, some even parked on the sidewalks, although no one ever seems to drive; people walk everywhere here.

"Come, sit back down with me." Ezra stands up and pulls Leeron sideways onto his lap. He wraps his freckled, muscular arms around her waist and nuzzles her shoulder. He swipes a dab of dark date juice from the underside of her pale, fine-boned jaw, then licks his finger.

David wakes from his nap, needing the bathroom. He tries to stand up, but even with the cane next to his chair, he's too weak. "Ezra," he calls feebly. "Ezra." They are still cuddled on the chaise, and the light on the balcony illuminates their faces. He's relieved Ezra seems so calm and gentle with Leeron. While Ezra did not inherit his looks, he did inherit his quick temper.

The first time David and Rachel realized that Ezra's anger was a problem was in the second grade, when Ezra tried to shove a classmate's finger into the pencil sharpener. They were horrified, but little Ezra defended himself, saying the classmate had pushed him out of the way when he had been patiently waiting in line. Nothing happened after that, until about a year later, when Ezra punched a child during recess. Again, they confronted him, and again he defended himself, saying the child was being mean to another friend.

After that incident, they enrolled Ezra in Tae Kwon Do, thinking that martial arts would help him channel his emotional energy properly. He excelled, but David never felt totally comfortable that Ezra wouldn't act on his anger. When he and Leeron started dating, David made sure to remind him that he must never, ever lay a hand on her.

David had made that mistake once, and it nearly cost him his marriage. He feels the bile in his throat thinking about it. He had grabbed Rachel by the arm one time when she was threatening to walk out of the apartment after a particularly heated argument. Only when she yanked herself away, crying, did he realize how hard he was holding her. She had black-and-blue marks on her arm for weeks. He winces at the memory, then calls again for Ezra to come help him up, but his feeble voice doesn't carry out to the balcony.

On the balcony, Ezra is reminiscing with Leeron about his father's crazy stories.

"Remember the time that psycho came first to his restaurant to eat and then shot up the people in the next stall? My father said it was a good thing the terrorist liked his food or he would be dead, too."

"Wait, which one—the terrorist or your father?"

"Good point," says Ezra, chuckling. "My father doesn't handle criticism of his food too well. He likes when people clean their plates."

"He's a good man."

"I know he is. That's part of why it's so hard to see him like this. He was always giving me advice: about girls, money, politics. Always telling me that food is the solution to everything, because people just want something good to eat. Let the Arab leaders come to his restaurant, and we'll have peace by the time the meal is done."

"As if it could be that easy!"

Ezra looks at his father lying asleep inside, and grabs Leeron's hand. "Let's move up the wedding. I'm worried my father won't live much longer."

Leeron furrows her forehead, then cocks her head. "To when?"

"This summer, right after you finish your army service."

"Let's see how he's doing after *Pesach* and then we'll talk. Nothing's happening before then, anyway."

Ezra leans in to kiss Leeron. "Okay, as long as you promise you'll marry me soon."

"I promise. But now I need to go. I'm so tired and I have to catch a bus back to the base. We'll see each other again in two weeks, right? Your commander promised to give you off for the first night of *Pesach?*"

"Yes, he promised. I told him this may be my father's last *Pesach* with us, so he relented. I guess he has a heart after all," says Ezra. "But two weeks is still a long time. Why don't I pick you up in the morning and take you to the bus?"

"That's sweet, but no," Leeron kisses him briefly and gives him a tight hug. "You have to catch your own bus, and you need sleep to have enough strength to load your tank. I'll see you very soon."

David feels a tapping on his shoulder. Ezra is gently trying to nudge him awake. He feels a wetness in his pants, and the mortification is a punch in the stomach. "I'm comfortable here. Don't move me. *Layla tov*."

***

A T *TAIM*, THE SASSOON restaurant, Manya Glassman sets the two small tables. In a matter of minutes, she sweeps the floor clean of the errant jellybeans and gummy worms that escaped from the neighboring candy stall, puts paper red-and-white-checked tablecloths and a box of napkins on each of the nine tables, and starts a pot of Turkish coffee. She slides open the glass door on the Coca-Cola branded refrigerator in the corner and loads in another six-pack of Goldstar beer bottles. Manya is old and bony, but strong from years of hard work. Her hair is a dull gray bob, pulled back on the sides with two black bobby pins, which makes her deeply lined, angular face look even more gaunt. She wears her usual blue-striped apron with snaps down the front and two deep pockets.

"Manya, how is it that no matter how early I try to get here, you always beat me to it?" Rachel asks.

"I do my best," murmurs Manya.

"Well, it's just going to be you and me again tonight, Manya. David isn't feeling well. Again. It's a good thing I have you to help me."

Rachel and David had planned to run the small restaurant on their own, but when Rachel became pregnant with Ezra, they hired Manya, a Polish-born child of Holocaust survivors. It seemed an unusual choice to David, to hire someone with zero background or taste for Iraqi food, but Rachel said she felt more comfortable with Manya than with any of the other waitresses they interviewed. In retrospect, David realized his flirtations with the pretty girls that worked at the neighboring stall hadn't gone unnoticed by Rachel, and Manya seemed far less threatening.

Manya didn't know much about Iraqi cuisine—the only spice in her mother's cooking was paprika—but she was quick, reliable, and hard-working. Also, she had a soft heart, especially for taxi drivers like her husband, Srulik. The Iraqi market was a popular place for pickup backgammon games—Srulik's favorite. While he had a regular game near the YMCA in the center of town, he frequently stopped by the *shuk* for an extra game if he was coming to drive Manya home.

It has become customary for anyone from Srulik's taxi company who stops by the counter to get a free cup of coffee. If they don't have enough money to pay for a full meal, Manya will take a few coins out of her own purse and deposit them in the cash register. Every night she packs a few family-size tins of leftover food to bring to the homeless people in Gan Hatoot.

Taim started as a lunch spot for workers, because David's time in the *ma'abara* left an indelible mark on him. As someone frugal and hardworking, he related better to those who labored with their hands than to those who worked in offices. Ironically, his restaurant has become a tourist hot spot, a "must eat!" on any *shuk* tasting tour.

It's a simple place, with a kitchen open to the dining area through a large pass-through window. Open shelves line the walls of the kitchen, holding stacks of plates and bowls, all in some shade of white. Trays of eggs in two-dozen cardboard cartons lie stacked precariously on the side of one of the inside counters. Along the main counter are twelve industrial-sized silver pots with big handles that sit on kerosene burners called *ptelias*, to allow the food to cook slowly. There are meatballs in a tomato and red pepper sauce, sofrito, beef goulash, stuffed cabbage, stuffed peppers, oxtail with rice and beans, and David's favorite: kubbeh soup (semolina dumplings filled with meat, in a lemony broth). Almost everything has some kind of liquid that can be mopped up by fresh pita bread, which the restaurant buys in bulk from the bakery around the corner.

Before David got too sick to go to the restaurant, he would spend most of his day there, delegating the food shopping to Rachel, the cleaning to Manya, and the cooking to himself. Once all the pots were bubbling, he would sit at his favorite table outside, engaging with the passersby and bantering with the neighboring workers.

"Dudi, *ma nishma*? How's the family?"

"Samir! Good to see you! How was the trip to Eilat?"

"Tzachi, are we playing ball later?"

He loved talking to his customers, both the regulars and the newcomers, and would spend time weaving throughout the tables, making sure everyone was well-fed and happy. If someone left food on his plate, David demanded an explanation. He took everything personally.

Taim used to only be open for lunch (which is the main meal of the day in Israel, and generally consists of some kind of meat), but now they're open for dinner, too, but with a limited menu. Some of the dishes that need to be slow cooked for hours sell out for the day with the lunch crowd and are then erased from the chalkboard menu. Saturday night is generally "appetizer-only" foods like olives, dips, pickles, *schnitzelonim* (breaded chicken fingers), and homemade hummus. Every restaurant in Israel claims to have the best hummus, but David's customers stand by his.

David still prepares his hummus at home, even when he's too tired to work at the restaurant. Once the chickpeas have soaked in water overnight, he mashes them with a mortar and pestle, leaving a few chickpeas whole for texture, then adds his secret ingredients, and spoons it all into a bowl. He'll drizzle a golden puddle of oil in the center, with some green parsley sprinkled on top. When he has the energy, he prepares a large tub, and Rachel brings it to the restaurant.

Tonight, however, Rachel comes empty-handed. David hasn't had the energy to make hummus in weeks. She'll have to make it herself. Rachel starts chopping parsley on one counter.

"How was your day, Manya? Did you do anything fun?"

"No."

Rachel turns on the radio. Manya was never one for conversation. Her husband Srulik loves to talk, and when he stops by the restaurant, he and Rachel confide in each other about their respective family health issues; Srulik and Manya's daughter, Yael, has cystic fibrosis. But tonight it's just the two women, and they work together in silence.

***

O N SUNDAY MORNING, DAVID and Rachel sit on the balcony of their apartment, drinking their second cup of coffee before Rachel has to go to the restaurant.

"I can't believe Ezra is still asleep," says Rachel. "It's hard for me to stay in bed for more than a few hours."

"He's exhausted from the training," says David. "I remember sleeping practically all through my time off when I was his age."

"Sometimes you still do." Rachel stands up and collects the empty cups.

David feels the familiar knot in his chest. Rachel's daily dig. He wonders if it's her way of coping with his illness, or how she gets out her anger towards him. Either way, it dissolves the rare good feeling he had a moment ago, enjoying being with Rachel while the morning sun filtered through the trees.

"I have to pick the girls up from Merav's house," says Rachel. "Then I'll head over to the restaurant. Do you think you'll be awake when Ezra goes back to base?"

David wants to give her the death stare, but he can't muster the strength. She has zapped everything from him. "I'll be awake."

He stays on the balcony for a long time, dozing on and off while listening to the news on the radio. Suddenly, his program is interrupted: "This is Roni Saban. We have reports of a terrorist attack. A bus has exploded on Route One, just outside the entrance to Jerusalem. At least eight people are dead, and many others wounded. The highway is closed in both directions."

David's stomach lurches, and he sits upright, rubbing his eyes and slapping his cheeks. He quickly goes through the list of family members in his head, thinking if any of them might be on the bus at this time. Rachel, Ezra, Ayelet, Shachar...no. His sisters are in Petach Tikva, so they should be okay. He allows himself to exhale, just a little. Having once witnessed the aftermath of a bus bombing on Jaffa Road, he can instantly imagine the devastating scene.

He pushes himself out of the chair, grabs his cane, and struggles to get inside to find his cell phone and call Rachel. As he comes through the balcony door, he hears it ringing.

"Have you talked to Ezra?"

"I don't know if he's awake yet. I just came into the house."

"I heard soldiers were killed in the bombing. Do you know names?"

David feels a tightening in his chest. He sits down on the couch and imagines Ezra in his olive-green army uniform, with his imposing, black Tavor assault rifle slung across his muscular chest. Even though Ezra is twenty-one years old and six feet tall, he is barely an adult. David has to remind himself that they have to send children to the army, because only teenagers feel invincible. He offers a silent prayer to God in thanks for Ezra's safety.

Then he walks down the hallway to Ezra's room, and sees him sitting on his bed, pale as a ghost and staring blankly.

"Ezra?"

Ezra looks at him with dull eyes. "Leeron is dead."

David feels a lump in his throat, threatening to choke him. "Leeron?" He sits next to Ezra on the bed.

"She was on the bus," he stammers. "She was killed instantly."

"Oh, no..." David puts his arm around Ezra, but Ezra shrinks away.

"Please go."

"Ezra..." David tries to pat his shoulder again.

Ezra jumps up and screams: "GO! OUT! NOW!"

***

LEERON HAS BEEN DEAD for only a few hours, but already it is time for her funeral. Jewish tradition dictates that the body is buried as quickly as possible out of respect for the deceased. The funeral is called for seven o'clock Sunday evening at the expansive *Har Hamenuchot* (Mountain of the Resting) cemetery by the Givat Shaul neighborhood.

It's the largest cemetery in Jerusalem, high on a hill, with undulating rows of simple limestone graves. There are no fancy mausoleums or ornate headstones. According to the Jewish tradition of human life going from "dust to dust," the dead are usually buried without coffins. However, victims of terror are always buried in coffins because their bodies often are not intact.

Ezra stands at the front, by the freshly dug grave, next to Leeron's parents and siblings. He wears sunglasses and a grimace, and has his hands balled up in fists in the front pockets of his jeans. Rachel stands on one side of him, and Ayelet and Shachar stand on the other. David feels too weak to stand, so he sits on a folding chair off to the side. He's embarrassed to be seen this way in public, a pathetic old man instead of a supportive father.

Rachel cries loudly. The rabbi recites Psalms and other prayers for Leeron until it's time for her to be interred. The men hold the stretcher above the grave, then pull out the long horizontal sheets of canvas that hold her coffin, careful to lower the box feet first. There is a thud as it hits the ground.

Now, the mourners take turns shoveling dirt into the grave. As the dirt lands on top of the coffin, it sounds like hail. When Ezra's friend Omer was killed near Lebanon a few summers ago,

Ezra didn't put down his shovel until every last bit of dirt had been laid on top of the grave. Now, he doesn't pick it up.

"Come Ezra," urges Rachel, handing him the shovel. "You have to do this. Do it for Leeron."

David pushes himself out of the chair and walks with his cane to the grave. He trades the cane for the shovel and struggles to lift a tiny bit of dirt. He tosses it into the grave and cringes at the sound. Ezra kneels down and puts his head between his legs.

Rachel crouches to the ground to meet his face.

"You need to get up." She pulls him up, hands him the shovel, and gently pushes him from the back so he is a step closer to the grave.

Ezra keeps his hands at his side, so David holds on to the shovel. Sweat is pouring off his brow. The dirt is so heavy, and he is tired. Finally, someone else takes the shovel and David staggers back to his chair.

***

T HE SASSOONS RETURN TO their apartment later that Sunday night. David's exhausted, barely able to make it through the front door and into their bedroom. Ayelet and Shachar go back to Merav's house. Ezra didn't utter a word the entire taxi ride home. He, too, goes straight to his room and shuts the door. Rachel quickly cleans up the morning dishes in the kitchen, takes two Xanax, and then, like her husband and son, heads to bed.

David lies awake, tossing and turning, listening to Rachel snore lightly, hoping that Ezra is sleeping, too. Ezra's door is closed and David knows, even if he felt up to it, he wouldn't dare go in.

He knows what it's like to deal with grief, especially the sudden death of a loved one. For David, it wasn't a girlfriend, but his cousin and closest friend, Judah, during the 1973 Yom Kippur War. The two of them were members of the same tank unit whose guard post on Tel Saki, a hill in the Southern Golan Heights, was attacked with barely any warning by the Syrian army. They were greatly outnumbered, but somehow David and five others survived.

Nowadays they treat soldiers like him, who have evaded death's grasp or witnessed violence and death, for PTSD. Today, David would be given medication, talk therapy, and who knows what else. But back then, he just bottled it all up inside. He still hates for Rachel to see him cry. Years ago, he never cried, but lately he tears up at nearly everything. It's the liver meds, he tells Rachel, though he's pretty sure she knows it's actually his fear, the sadness of his own impending death, and the burden of memory becoming heavier with age.

It pains him to remember how he pushed Rachel away after he returned from war. He drank, he smoked, they had rough sex. She encouraged him to talk, but Israeli men don't talk.

Then there was the road rage incident, when he nearly ran their car off a cliff. That changed things for him. Rachel threatened to leave him unless he would at least take some anti-anxiety medication. And all the while, they were going through their infertility problem. Had that been God's way of saying he wasn't worthy? In the end, it was a blessing because more years had passed from the war to when Ezra was born, and by then the emotional scars had thickened, and he was more patient.

David takes a deep breath, resigned to being awake. He worries that not only will he not be able to fill the void of Leeron's absence, but also that he won't be able to keep Ezra calm the way she did. He struggles to think of the right things to say to his son, how to protect him from letting his grief turn into anger and violence.

***

A BIT LATER, DAVID's cell phone rings.

"David, it's Yoni. I have amazing news—we have a liver for you."

Stunned silence.

"David?"

David opens his mouth but can't speak. Dr. Yoni Bardash is a childhood friend of his from primary school and has been his hepatologist since he got sick. He maintains a professional relationship with Rachel, but when he speaks to David, it is as if they are both ten years old again. "David, are you there?"

Rachel grabs the phone. "Hello?"

"Rachel, it's Yoni. We have a liver for David!"

Rachel sucks in her breath. "Oh, my God. What? How? I can't..."

"Rachel, what's wrong? This is amazing news!"

"Oh Yoni, it's so awful. You remember Ezra's longtime girlfriend Leeron? She was killed this morning in a suicide bombing."

"Oh, my God."

"They wanted to get married."

"Rachel, I have to tell you something," says Yoni in a quiet voice. "I really shouldn't be telling you this, but I think it will help you deal with things."

"What are you talking about?"

"The liver that we have for you is from one of the victims of the same suicide bombing that killed Leeron."

"What? How can this be?" Rachel is shaking now. "Wait—it's not from Leeron, is it? Tell me it's not from Leeron!"

"It's not from Leeron."

"Oh my God—it is from the bomber? Tell me it's not from the bomber! I think if it's from the bomber we have to say no. Oh God, David will die! But we have to say no! How can the person who killed Leeron be a part of David?"

"You need to calm down and breathe." Yoni is stern. "I promise you, the liver is not from Leeron and it's not from the bomber. It's from another innocent victim, another Jew. You need to get yourself together and get David to Hadassah Ein Kerem hospital as soon as possible so we can prep him for surgery. I know it's terrible timing, Rachel, but this is good news."

Rachel hangs up the phone and she and David embrace. David leans his head on her shoulder and cries heaving, wracking sobs.

"Is this a dream?"

Rachel rubs David's back and helps him to sit on the edge of the bed. "It's a dream and a nightmare all at once."

"I would have gladly traded places with Leeron," he says. "I loved her like a daughter."

"I know you did. I did, too. She was pure gold."

Tears continue streaming down Rachel's face. She staggers into the kitchen, turns on the sink, bends her head underneath the faucet, and gulps water. It splashes down her chin and onto her chest.

She dials Manya's number.

"Hello? Manya? It's Rachel. I'm sorry for calling so late."

"I'm awake." Manya's voice is calm and quiet.

"Manya, I don't know who else to talk to. I...something has happened..." Rachel starts to cry. She sobs into the phone for a minute, then takes a deep breath. "Manya, are you still there?"

"I'm listening."

Rachel tells Manya everything that has transpired over the past twelve hours. "How can it be that this bombing killed the love of Ezra's life but will save the love of my life?"

"God is mysterious," says Manya. "We have no answers. Go take care of your husband and your son, and I will take care of the restaurant." She says goodbye and hangs up.

Rachel knocks on Ezra's door. There is no answer. She gently opens it. His bed is empty, and his phone lies on the floor.

***

E ZRA HAS BEEN RUNNING in the dark for nearly an hour. He heads away from the center of town, through the residential neighborhoods of Baka and the German Colony, down Derech Hebron to the industrial area of Talpiot. It hasn't rained in more than a month and puffs of dust from the limestone sidewalks swirl in the air with every stride he takes, turning the hair on his legs a light gray color. Ezra is sweaty, with no water, no money, and no phone. Suddenly he stops and vomits all over the sidewalk. He slumps down on the curb and leans his head between his knees.

When he finally musters the strength to stagger back to his family's apartment on Agrippas, he avoids the chaos of Machane Yehuda by going through the little maze of alleyways and one-way streets littered with stray cats and hanging laundry. He walks part of the way with his eyes closed. He still feels lightheaded and faint.

Ezra opens the door to the empty apartment and heads straight for the kitchen. He gulps some orange juice from the refrigerator, then goes to his room to undress. He checks his phone. Missed calls from his mother. Missed calls from his father. And a text from his mother: "There's a liver for *Abba*! We're at Hadassah Ein Kerem."

For a moment, Ezra stands in stunned silence, staring at his phone. Then he whoops out loud, before bursting into wracking sobs. After a few minutes, he smacks himself on both cheeks, pulls on jeans and a t-shirt, and lifts his mattress to get his rifle. Army regulations dictate that a soldier must have his weapon on him at all times, even when on leave. All over Israel, soldiers in and out of uniform walk around with guns slung across their bodies. Ezra keeps his gun with him most of the time, but when he goes running, he hides his gun under his mattress. He puts the shoulder strap diagonally across his chest, with his gun hanging across his back. The buttstock is pointed down, and the orange safety plug in the chamber is clearly noticeable.

Meanwhile, David and Rachel have just arrived at Hadassah Ein-Kerem Medical Center. They are sitting in the waiting area of the emergency department, as the main admissions area is closed for the night. Among the other people waiting are a Haredi Jewish family with five girls, all in matching navy dresses, huddled together in the corner; a bearded man with dark hair sitting against one wall with two teenage boys crouched next to him; and a robed priest pacing the floor.

Rachel whispers to David under her breath, "What are all of these people doing here in the middle of the night?"

But David can't speak. The buzz of Hebrew, English, and Arabic chatter around him are making it hard for him to concentrate over his feelings of excitement and fear. What if this works? What if he'll be a normal person again? Be able to work, be useful. He looks at Rachel and vows to himself that he'll be a better husband.

And yet he also worries that if the transplant fails, he won't get another chance. Yoni said his liver functioning is worsening; if it took this long to get a donor, it's unlikely another liver will come along.

"Do you think any of these people are still waiting for those hurt in today's bombing?" Rachel asks. "The dead are gone, but so many were injured."

The lump in David's throat thickens again, and he swallows and tries to breathe shallowly. He can't let himself think about the bombing. Rachel told him that he's getting a liver from one of the victims, and he keeps thinking about Leeron. He can't fathom how her family is coping. And his donor...his lifesaver...why does he deserve to live and this person die? It's unfathomable.

A nurse calls David's name, brings over a wheelchair, and escorts David and Rachel upstairs. Shortly after they leave, Ezra arrives. The nurse tells him that he just missed them, and he will have to wait. There are only a few empty chairs, so he grabs one opposite a Haredi Jewish family. Ezra jiggles his knees up and down, wiping his sweaty palms on his thighs, trying to take deep breaths.

Suddenly, he's choking on his own saliva. Sweat pours off his forehead. His heart is pounding. He can't take a deep breath. Ezra jumps out of his seat and bolts out the door.

With glazed eyes and a wild, frantic look, he starts jogging up the block towards the wide, four-lane boulevard across the street to the hospital. His gun is slung over his shoulder, and he's looking down at the sidewalk, muttering to himself.

At the same time, two teenage Arab boys are running just ahead of him. A group of soldiers are yelling at the boys to stop.

Ezra snaps his head up. The two teenagers are just a few hundred feet ahead of him.

"I've got them!" he shouts to the soldiers. To the boys he screams: "Stop!"

The boys keep running.

Ezra runs after them. "Stop!"

One of the boys stumbles on a rock, and loses his footing just as Ezra stops, shoulders his rifle, flicks the safety, aims low, and shoots.

Pancreas

"HOLY MARY MOTHER OF God!" While bounding down the stairs of the hospital parking lot on Saturday morning, Father Severin McConnell misses a step and rolls his ankle. He winces from the searing pain, crashing to the ground with a groan as his brown robe pools around him like a puddle of mud.

"I thought priests weren't supposed to say that kind of thing," says an older, bearded man from the top of the stairs. He climbs down and crouches next to Severin.

"Dr. Yeleved! Shalom! I, uh...." Severin reddens and pushes his gold wire glasses back up on his nose. "I was rushing to the emergency department, and I wasn't watching my step."

"It's okay, Father. I was just joking." Dr. Yeleved puts Severin's arm around his shoulder and helps him up.

Severin smacks the dust off his robe with both hands, then ties the cincture around his waist. He pats down his thinning brown hair and wipes the thin layer of sweat off his forehead. It feels like summer even though it's early April. Gingerly, he sets his sandaled foot to the ground.

"Can you put weight on it?"

"Yes, it's fine. I'm okay."

"Then let's get you inside and check your blood sugar. You must be low."

Severin wills himself not to react. He knows Dr. Yeleved is only trying to be helpful, but he wishes not everyone at the hospital would consider themselves Severin's doctor.

Unfortunately, Severin's unstable diabetic condition has brought him more celebrity than his near-decade of volunteering as a medical clown.

"No, I'm okay, for once. It's just my ankle." He shows Dr. Yeleved the blood glucose reading on his phone, then reaches out to shake Dr. Yeleved's hand. "Thank you for your help."

"Thank you, Father, for your constant volunteering. Everyone at Shaare Zedek appreciates how often you give your time. Especially the kids."

"And I appreciate how kind everyone is to the diabetic priest," Severin says. "I must've fainted on every floor of this hospital. The Church certainly found the perfect place for me to do my lay service."

"Well, at least you usually have on your clowning costume, so it seems part of your act." Dr. Yeleved claps him on the shoulder. "I have to run. Feel good!"

Twice a week for the past decade, Severin dons overalls, a polka-dotted shirt, rainbow wig, and red nose, and parades through the hospital, entertaining the patients. He started out only visiting pediatric patients, but when he saw the smiles from adults as he walked through the other floors in his get-up, he realized he could be a source of enjoyment for all ages.

The only problem is his fainting. His diabetes is poorly controlled, despite a continuous glucose monitor, medication, and his strict low-sugar, low-carbohydrate diet. Severin suffers from hypoglycemic unawareness, a dangerous side effect of diabetes when blood glucose can drop with little or no warning, causing fainting, or even seizures and coma.

A pancreas transplant would cure his diabetes, his doctor says. The pancreas is an organ about the size of a hand that lies in the lower part of the stomach. One of its functions is to help digest food and to provide hormones such as insulin that maintain optimal blood sugar levels to help the body use and store energy for food. Only a brain-dead person can donate a pancreas, so it could take a few years for a pancreas to become available.

Severin hopes he won't have to wait that long to be healthy. He needs to be well now, so that he can adopt little Hadas, a sickly, premature baby that was abandoned by her biological parents. He smiles just thinking about seeing her later up in the Newborn Intensive Care Unit (NICU). But first, he needs to go be a chaplain in the emergency department.

On Saturdays, the waiting area is a crapshoot: sometimes it's empty, sometimes it's packed. Shaare Zedek Medical Center is in the southwestern part of Jerusalem where many religious Jews live, and on the Sabbath, the emergency department is generally more quiet than other days. The emergency department is three levels underground, as are the main operating theaters, pharmacy, and medical supply center, so that the hospital can function normally even under military attack. As one of the main area hospitals, trauma victims are often sent here, and Severin still has nightmares from ministering to terror victims of a suicide bombing in a pizzeria many years ago.

Although he has lived in Jerusalem for more than twenty years, Severin is still uncomfortable with the threatening undercurrent of violence at any moment. Jerusalem is a far cry from his upbringing in rural Ireland in practically every way. It's crowded and noisy and dusty, and the smells of food and people are overwhelming. Only the feeling of being an outsider seems similar. There, as an orphan; here, as a Christian.

Severin knows it's his religious duty to help people in need, so he sits in the emergency waiting room for an hour a week. It's another of God's magic tricks, he thinks, that strengthening others mitigates his fears.

Normally, Severin wears his long, hooded monk's robe with a corded rope, as is common for all members of the Franciscan Order. Founded by St. Francis of Assisi in the thirteenth century, the Order espouses a life of poverty, humility, and service to the community. While many men in Jerusalem are dressed in religious garb, it is usually either the black hats and long overcoats of the Hasidic Jews, or the white *thobe* (robe) and *ghutra* (headscarf) of the Muslims. Christians represent just a tiny percentage of the Israeli population, and the primary work of Severin's monastery is the *"Custodia Terra Sancta"*—to guard the Christian holy places here.

On this Saturday morning, there is only one person in the emergency waiting area, a middle-aged Arab woman. She's wearing a purple hijab and a matching djaballa, while sitting on a chair looking at her phone. Severin sits down near her.

"Hi, I'm Father Severin. Is there anything I can do to help you? Or would you just like some company?"

The woman glances sideways at him and looks back down at her phone.

Severin asks again, this time in Arabic.

"No, thank you," she says and moves to a chair on the opposite side of the room.

Severin sighs and reads his Breviary (prayers for the day), trying to shrug off the sting of rejection. While he's used to being rebuffed, every person that refuses to engage reopens the childhood scab from sitting alone in the school lunchroom. But most people are friendly and willing to at least make small talk. There have been a few times that Severin has made real friends here, and it's those personal connections that fortify him. Without any family of his own, Severin always tries to form bonds with others.

"Hi Father Severin!" The bearded janitor interrupts his reverie, swishing his mop between the priest's feet.

"Tomer! How are you?"

"Doing well, Father, doing well. You're headed up to do the clown thing?"

"Later, yes," Severin stands up to get out of the way of the mop. "But first I'm heading up to the NICU. I'm a baby cuddler."

"A baby cuddler!" Tomer laughs. "That sounds like a good job. I could hold my babies all day."

Severin gives a wistful smile. "You're a good father, Tomer."

"Not just a father! I'm a grandfather now, too." Tomer pulls out his phone and shows Severin a picture. "My daughter had a baby boy a few months ago. Look how adorable he is."

Severin forces a smile on his face to hide his feelings of jealousy. "Good for you, Tomer. Well, I need to be going." Severin limps down the linoleum hallway to the elevator bank and presses the button.

"Now you can pretend to be a father, Father." Tomer laughs. Severin jams his thumb repeatedly on the button. It's the oldest and worst joke in the book. Why can't he be a Father and a father?

Alone in the elevator, he remembers confiding his wish to adopt baby Hadas to Annette, a NICU nurse who is one of his parishioners at San Savior Monastery, where he works and lives. He had never admitted it to anyone before—in fact, he had only recently admitted it to himself—but he and Annette have developed a deeper friendship over the last few months since he's been volunteering in the NICU, and he felt comfortable opening up to her. To his relief, she immediately encouraged him to pursue adoption.

"Hadas will be the luckiest kid in the world!" She reached out to him with open arms as if to hug him, but quickly slapped her hands together in an exaggerated clapping motion. "You're kind, patient, funny...way better than my own father was."

"Well, I never had a father, so I guess anything is better than nothing," joked Severin.

"And she's already bonded with you," said Annette. "You've been with her practically since the day she was born."

"I do feel connected to her already." He lowered his voice to a whisper. "But I can't adopt a child if I'm a priest. I'll have to leave the ministry."

"Oh, my...no!" cried Annette. She immediately blushed. "I mean...never mind me. You should do what's best for you. I'll just miss listening to your sermons and all that."

"It's not a decision I take lightly," said Severin, tapping his heart. "My whole life is and has been the Church, but I have to figure out if that's all my life is meant to be."

When the elevator opens on the sixth floor, Severin exits slowly, trying not to put much weight on his sore ankle. His mood lightens as he approaches the NICU. It's prettier than many of the other wards in the hospital. The floor is a warm brown wood, rather than ugly green linoleum, and each of the twenty cubicles has a pastel-colored square painted behind it, creating a beautiful watercolor theme. The isolettes have the requisite monitors and wires, but the curtain separators are in a teddy-bear print, and each area has its own seafoam-green rocking chair with a soft white throw blanket draped on its arm.

Severin admires the hospital's effort to make the NICU look soothing. It must feel like anything but to the parents. The bright lights and constant beeping of the alarms are still frightening to him, even after being there regularly for three months. The babies are so tiny in their incubators, you can hardly see them. From afar, they look like a jumble of machines and cords. In fact, the first time he held Hadas, he felt like he was holding a bundle of wires swaddled in a blanket, rather than an actual baby.

Thank God she's put on some weight, and there's no mistaking her for electronics anymore. When he first met Hadas, she weighed only 538 grams—just a little over one pound. She was born fifteen-weeks premature to a young mother who had abused alcohol and drugs and had zero prenatal care. Doctors warned her mother that Hadas would likely have severe medical problems and might not even survive, but she insisted they do everything possible to save her baby. Yet after Hadas's mother was discharged from the hospital, she disappeared, and the hospital has been unable to contact her. After three months, Hadas is now officially considered "abandoned," and is a ward of the state.

***

ANNETTE FIRST APPROACHED SEVERIN in early January, right after Sunday Mass, and asked if he wanted to be a special volunteer for the NICU. The hospital had a regular baby cuddler program for NICU babies whose parents visited but couldn't be in the hospital frequently enough because of their work or family obligations. Being a "special" volunteer meant that Severin would spend time caring for the same baby every time (so they would form a bond), and meant he would have to commit to coming at least twice a week for three hours.

"I don't know anything about babies," Severin protested. "Why are you asking me?"

"Because you're kind. And there's not much to know. You just need to hold her."

"Would the hospital trust me with babies, considering my fainting?" Severin asked.

"Everyone in the hospital knows and loves you," said Annette, reassuringly. "I need you to start tomorrow. Hadas is only a week old, but she hasn't had any visitors, and she needs someone to give her love. We're too busy in the NICU to just sit and rock the babies."

Severin was tasked with holding the baby, singing and talking to her, and calming her during any medical procedures she might need to undergo. Annette warned him that Hadas was very small and very sick. She was attached to a ventilator to help her breathe, and the tape securing it to her face covered nearly everything but her eyes. She was having seizures as part of her withdrawal from the heroin she was exposed to in utero, and she was hard to console.

"She's not going to look anything like you imagine a newborn baby would," said Annette. "But the more you hold her and soothe her, the better she'll feel. You will literally be saving her life."

It only took Annette two days to secure permission for Severin to come into the NICU. The first time he went to work as a baby cuddler, it was freezing cold outside, and he was shivering when he first arrived at the NICU, both from the winter weather and from the fear that he would do something wrong, or faint while holding her.

"You're going to do great," Severin heard a voice from behind him say. He turned to face a tall, older woman dressed in scrubs and a surgical cap, who smiled and waved to him. "Hi, I'm Penina, another NICU nurse. Annette told me you'd be here today to spend some time cuddling Hadas. I had a feeling you'd get here early, so I went and got us both some coffee. Here you go."

Severin took the cup and thanked her. "Aren't you scared of breaking them?" he asked, looking through the window at the babies.

"No, and neither should you be," Penina said. She adjusted her surgical cap, tucking in a stray gray hair from the nape of her neck. "These babies need all the love they can get."

"Did Annette tell you about my hypoglycemic unawareness?"

"She did. We're going to check your blood sugar right now, and you're going to be sitting in a rocking chair most of the time, anyway."

Penina handed Severin a yellow hospital gown to put over his monk's robe, along with a blue disposable surgical cap for his head.

"*Yalla*, let's go," said Penina, holding open the door. "I have to help prep one of the babies for a procedure this morning, so Annette is going to get you started."

Inside the NICU, the cacophony of beeps and alarms dispelled whatever notions Severin had about it being a peaceful setting. He felt a knot forming in his stomach.

"Hi Father Sev! I'm so glad you made it this morning," said the short woman with thick glasses and big dimples, smiling widely at him from across the room.

"Hi Annette!" Severin waved hello. "Can we say a prayer before we start?"

"Of course!"

"May all the beautiful children here be wrapped up in God's love, found deep in His everlasting wings. Carried and kept, safe and cherished. May the healing power of Christ breathe across their beings now."

"Amen," said Annette.

"No offense, but I don't believe in God," said Penina. "My mother survived the Holocaust only to die of ovarian cancer when my brother and I were young children. How could God exist and allow those things?"

Severin pursed his lips. He looked around the room at the isolettes, listening to the newborns' soft grunting, thinking to himself, "Each baby is a miracle," and wondering how a person could work in a place like this and not believe in God. But he kept quiet.

"You're not religious?" Annette asked Penina, incredulously. "But you always wear skirts like the religious Jews."

"That's for these wide hips of mine. Skirts are more comfortable. No other reason."

Severin cleared his throat. "So, when can I meet Hadas?"

Penina's face softened, and she smiled at Severin. "Thank you for changing the subject."

"I appreciate that, although I feel quite nervous right now."

"Don't be," said Annette. She led Severin to an incubator in the back of the room. Hadas was lying on her back, eyes closed, wearing just a diaper. Her papery skin had an orange tinge to it, and a fine layer of light, downy hair. A breathing tube secured with surgical tape covered her mouth and part of her tiny nose. Two electrode pads were stuck to her chest, atop her jutting ribs, and there was a PICC (peripherally inserted central catheter) line in a vein of her left arm. Her limbs were as tiny as toothpicks, but Severin was amazed to count ten fingers and toes, perfectly formed, albeit in miniature.

He peered at the baby. "What a wee lass!"

"You should have seen her a week ago—she was even tinier!" Annette pointed to the sink. "Go wash your hands for thirty seconds, then put on a pair of those purple gloves."

Annette led Severin to a partitioned area with glass walls on the left side of the NICU and patted the rocking chair. "Now, come sit here. Penina said you need to check your blood sugar first?"

Severin took out his phone. "I have a continuous glucose monitor under the skin of my stomach, and it sends readings to my phone every five minutes." He pressed a button. "I'm good."

"Must be very hard to have hypoglycemic unawareness, ay?"

Severin nodded his head. "I don't feel anything wrong, but then I just faint. I tried an insulin pump, but I hated how it felt. My doctor said the only thing that will help is a pancreas transplant. I'm desperate to be healthy."

"Is everything else okay? Your kidneys? Your eyesight?"

"For now, yes, praise the Lord. But my doctor worries about all these things, especially as I get older. Diabetes is sneaky and insidious. Suddenly you can go from okay to terrible. What would be amazing about a transplant is that it would actually cure me of diabetes."

Annette nodded. "I hope you'll get a new pancreas soon, Father Sev. In the meantime, let's get baby Hadas."

She placed a pillow on Severin's lap. "This will make it more comfortable for both of you. And it will make it safer if you suddenly feel unsteady."

Severin's stomach spasmed again. He had never held a baby this small before. The babies he normally held during baptisms seemed enormous compared to Hadas.

Annette unswaddled Hadas from her blanket and gently placed her in Severin's arms. She lay the attached wires over the armrest and tucked in the ends of Hadas' pink blanket to keep her wrapped up. Severin stroked the top of the baby's right cheek, marveling at how warm and soft it was, while at the same time wincing at the sight of the tape covering most of her face. He bent his head down and inhaled her sweet baby scent, and for a moment he couldn't smell the strong disinfectant that permeated the whole hospital.

His chest swelled with an overwhelming love so powerful that it hurt and felt unlike anything he had ever experienced before. Severin had just met this child, but suddenly he cared about her more than anything in the world. He felt tears welling up in his eyes.

"You're a natural. I should send a picture to your mother."

"I don't have a mother."

"I'm sorry." Annette cleared her throat. "When did she die?"

"I don't actually know...it's a complicated story." The rhythmic rising of Hadas's chest slowed Severin's heart rate, like the soothing tick-tock of a metronome. He could still hear the beeping and alarm sounds from the main room, although they were muffled by the glass wall. "Do you have to check those alarms?"

"Trying to get rid of me, ay?"

Severin blushed. "Not at all! I just..."

"I'm joking with you, Father." Annette knocked on the glass and held up one finger to Penina. "Penina has control of everything right now, and there are two parent visitors here, as well. I'll pop in there in a minute, and when I come back, you can tell me your story."

"I don't really have much to tell," said Severin. "Honestly, I wish I could just make something up, but I try not to lie."

As Annette slid open the glass partition, Severin sighed with relief. He rarely talked about his childhood. It wasn't something he liked to think about, let alone discuss. The truth was, he didn't remember much about his very early years, but he was told by the nuns that his unwed mother left him at the orphanage when he was just a few days old. By the time he was old enough to ask questions, his mother and his grandparents were dead.

He looked down at Hadas and tried to imagine how his own mother felt, gazing at his face in the same way. Did she hold him like this? Did she breastfeed him, even once? Or did she abandon him with seemingly no thought or concern for his future? He wondered what would happen with Hadas.

***

THAT JANUARY NIGHT, AFTER holding Hadas for the first time, Severin felt the opposite of how he had in the morning. Despite the cold, he felt warm inside. Instead of nervous butterflies in his stomach, he felt a lovely fluttering in his chest. He couldn't wait to get back to the monastery and tell Friar Michael Pelgon—his roommate and best friend—all about it.

The San Savior Monastery is a large compound located at One Saint Francis Street, east of the New Gate, within the

Christian Quarter in the Old City of Jerusalem. Although it is not considered the holiest Christian site—that's the Church of the Sepulchre, where Jesus was said to have been crucified, and later buried and resurrected—it has special status as being the "Custodian of the Holy Land," or *Custodia Terra Sancta*. These offices are part of the compound, as are the church, dormitory, printing press (publishing house), organ workshop, library, Catholic school, and museum. Built in 1559, the chapel has high, vaulted ceilings with marble pillars, giant, gleaming organ pipes, and rows of wooden pews that have a warm glow from centuries of use.

Generally, senior members sleep in the same room as junior members, either all in one big dormitory, or in small groups spread throughout different rooms. For many years, Severin slept in a large room with many other monks, but his continuous glucose monitor woke others in the night when his alarms sounded, so he moved into the small bedroom in the hallway leading to the clock tower, which had previously been used for visitors.

One night, Severin didn't wake up from his Dexcom alarm. When he failed to show up for morning services, Friar Michael, his close friend and a fellow Irishman, went to his room to check on him and found him in bed, unconscious. After Michael helped rush him to the hospital, he was told they had gotten there just in time. A few more hours, and Severin might have fallen into a coma, or worse.

Since then, to accommodate Severin's medical situation, Michael has shared his room. The space is tight, with barely enough room for two twin beds separated by a night table, a small desk, and a chair. The walls are plastered a dull ivory white, unadorned except for a large wooden cross that hangs over Severin's bed. Severin is a notoriously deep sleeper, and Michael is responsible for waking up if the Dexcom alarm sounds, and helping Severin either to take insulin, if his blood sugar is too high, or, if it's too low—as is usually the case—to eat some of the jelly beans stashed in the night-table drawer.

As soon as Severin and Michael were alone in their bedroom that night, Severin told him about baby Hadas. "I had the most wonderful experience today. I was at the hospital, as usual, but this time I helped take care of the tiniest newborn, no bigger than my hand. She was so soft and sweet, and my whole job is just to give her some love and attention."

Michael laughed. "That sounds nice, but what do you know about babies?"

"I worried about the same thing, but it just felt natural. I loved it."

"How interesting. Well, it still seems like a very strange job for a priest."

"Perhaps, but the nurses said I was good at it, and I'll have to go back a few times a week to help out." The conversation wasn't going at all like Severin had thought it would. Michael seemed disinterested and even a bit discouraging.

Severin is fifteen years older than Michael, and when they first met, he treated him as a younger brother, serving as both guide and mentor. But when they became roommates, their friendship deepened. They talked late into the night, and Severin opened up to Michael about his childhood, the loneliness he felt as an orphan. Michael told Severin about his father's alcoholism and how he got the scar on his temple from a smashed beer bottle, and they bonded over their deep grief.

"If you think that's the right way to do your lay service, dedicating so much time to just one baby, then go ahead," Michael said in a clipped tone. For the life of him, Severin couldn't understand why.

"This baby could die without enough care," he said. "I'm going to do whatever the nurses tell me. We'll see how long Hadas needs help."

***

B Y NOW, SEVERIN ALREADY knows he'll need to visit Hadas for the foreseeable future. Her mother is unlikely to return. She left Hadas at the hospital the day after giving birth, and they haven't been able to contact her since. There are no other known relatives. Child protective services will be taking Hadas as a ward of the state as soon as she is able to leave the hospital, which could be months, or even a year away. Depending on her health, she could go to a foster or adoptive home, or she might have to be institutionalized at an orphanage.

Severin has been thinking of adopting Hadas for a while now. He has already confided in Annette and told Penina, as well, knowing he would need both of them to advocate for him. The thought of her living in an orphanage the way he did breaks his heart. He can't understand how people can abandon their babies. At least in his case—he hopes—his mother didn't want to leave him but was forced to because she was unmarried. And that's the reason she killed herself—or that's the story he always tells himself.

Up in the NICU, Hadas, wearing just a diaper, sleeps soundly against Severin's bare chest. He started "kangaroo cuddling" the second time he came to hold Hadas, Annette having explained to him that skin-to-skin contact has been scientifically shown to improve a baby's health. It isn't clear whether it's the body warmth, or the sound of the adult heartbeat, or just the extreme closeness. Severin was bashful initially, but as he saw all the parent visitors to the NICU shedding their shirts, he became more comfortable.

Hadas's tiny hands are clenched into fists. He gently pokes his finger into one of them to try to unfurl her fingers. Immediately, Hadas grabs onto Severin's finger and holds it tight. Even though Severin tries to resist, this moves him to tears.

He can remember only one time when a nun hugged him, after he stepped on a beehive and was stung thirty times on his feet and legs. The nuns were strict with discipline and miserly with affection, although they weren't as abusive the way they were in some of the other, more notorious orphanages in Ireland.

"Are you okay there, Father Sev?" Annette crouches down in front of him.

"What a sweet baby," says Severin, blinking his eyes. "She's barely bigger than my hand."

"Ay, and when they're this little, they just jab you right in the heart, don't they?"

Penina wheels an empty isolette back into the side room and parks it in the open area. "Am I dreaming, or do you both become more Irish speaking with each other?

"We're like a bunch of leprechauns about to break into the Riverdance," says Severin. "I'm just joking. You're right—I do find my accent becomes stronger when talking with other Mc-Doogles."

"With what?" Penina snorts.

"Other Irishmen," answers Severin. "I'm surprised you haven't learned any Irish slang despite working with Annette for so long."

"No, I haven't, and she hasn't learned any Hebrew slang, either," says Penina. "They teach you proper grammar and language in the immigrant *ulpan*, but not how to talk like a hip Israeli."

"Where's the hip Israeli?" Annette asks. Penina swats her arm with a diaper cloth.

"I may be the oldest one here, but I am hip. Just ask my grandchildren."

"Father Sev, you've never told us how you got from Ireland to Israel," says Annette.

"That's a quick one: I had an aptitude for languages, I was a good monk, and I was an orphan."

BEEP! Another monitor sounds by the door. Annette and Penina look at each other.

"I'll get that," says Penina.

Severin adjusts himself in the chair, and one of Hadas's wires moves. BEEP!

"Oh no, did I do something wrong?" Severin's heart thumps.

"Nothing at all, Father Sev. You've got to relax. After three months, I thought you'd be used to the machines already." Annette adjusts the wire so it's tucked under the pillow on Severin's lap. "Are you still okay sitting there like this? You can take a break if you need."

Severin looks tenderly at Hadas. "I could stay like this for hours."

"You'll be a great father," says Penina, who came back and is now inputting information into the computer next to Severin. "But raising a child alone is hard. My father was very lonely, and he had an especially hard time with me starting around age ten when I really needed a woman around."

Severin nods his head. "I don't really have a plan yet, because it seems like a pipe dream. I can't adopt a baby unless I'm healthy. I've been on the waiting list for a pancreas for nineteen months already, and no luck yet."

"Why do you want to adopt Hadas?" asks Penina.

Annette wags her finger at Penina. "I'm sorry, Father. Jews are not like us—they love to ask questions. I have to go check on Baby Orli. I'll be right back."

Penina puts her hand on her chest. "What? Am I being intrusive?"

"No, it's fine," Severin answers. "I feel such a strong connection to her, and it has made me realize that I want to be part of a family."

He clears his throat and continues. "Growing up, I didn't know anything about either of my parents. When I asked questions, I was just told that no one knew who my father was, and that my mother had disappeared. By the time I was old enough to look up my birth records, my mother had died. Suicide."

He takes a deep breath. "And now the sisters are gone, too. I'm alone, and I want a family of my own."

"Can you have a child if you're a priest?"

Severin shakes his head. "No. That's one of the things holding me back. That, and my unstable health."

Seeing tears on his face, Penina sits down next to him. "Do you need a break?"

"No, I'm fine," says Severin. "Anyway, I feel terrible that you and Annette take time to check on me. I know you're so busy."

"Don't be silly—it takes barely a minute. And if you weren't here, no one would be holding Hadas. While I'd love to hold her all day, I'm too busy. And then unfortunately babies like Hadas who don't get many visitors just lie alone."

"It breaks my heart."

Penina nods. "The worst thing in the world is when a baby never cries. You might think it's a good thing, but really, it means the baby learned that even when she cries, no one comes, so what's the point?"

Severin is quiet. Maybe when the nuns always told him he never cried, it didn't mean he was a content, easy baby, as he had always thought.

Penina gets up to leave, then says to Severin: "Actually, that's not even the worst thing. What kills me the most inside is that I'm the one who makes the baby suffer. I'm the one who has to poke and prod and cause pain to this tiny being, and a lot of the time, it's for nothing. The baby will die anyway because it was born too early, with too many complicated medical problems. But if the parent—who is now totally absent, by the way—said at delivery to do everything to save the baby, we have no choice but to keep going. It's torture."

"It's all in God's hands," says Severin. "But I can understand how hard it is for you, and I admire your strength."

As he kisses the top of Hadas's head again, Severin wonders if he would be able to stick a needle into the inside of her tiny wrist. And what if he had been a sickly child? Would the nuns have cared for him as he needed? If he had diabetes then, he probably wouldn't be alive now.

Annette returns to the cubicle and extends her arms. "Time for me to take Hadas, and for you to go have lunch, Father."

Severin squeezes Hadas as tightly as he dares. "I hate to leave her."

"You need to take care of yourself. Eat something, and get that ankle checked out," says Annette, sternly. "No medical clowning for you today. I'll see you at Mass tomorrow."

Severin reluctantly lowers Hadas to the pillow, and Annette takes her back to her isolette.

"I'll see you again soon," he says.

"Absolutely!" Penina and Annette answer in unison, then burst into laughter.

"We spend too much time together," grumbles Penina with a wide smile.

Severin leans over Hadas's isolette. "Goodbye, sweet girl. Be brave and strong."

***

SEVERIN USUALLY WALKS OR takes the bus back to the San Savior monastery, but on Saturdays the buses don't run in Jerusalem, in observance of the Sabbath. It's a long walk to the Old City from Shaare Zedek, so occasionally he takes a taxi, or gets a ride from his friend Srulik Glassman. When Severin first arrived in Israel from Ireland twenty-two years ago, Srulik happened to be his taxi driver from the airport. He was the first Israeli that Severin had ever met, and the first Jew. They quickly figured out that they could speak to each other most easily in French—Severin had studied French as a boy and Srulik was born in France. By the time they got to the monastery in Jerusalem, the two had exchanged phone numbers, and a decades-long friendship ensued. Severin felt bad taking rides from Srulik, as he not only stopped accepting payment but also was now an old man of about eighty years old.

Today, though, his ankle hurts too much for the hour-long walk back home, so he calls Srulik for a ride. He knows that as a secular Jew, Srulik does not strictly observe the Sabbath.

"Srulik, how are you, my friend?"

"My favorite priest! I'm good. How are you?"

"I'm good, but I need to ask you for a favor. Are you busy?"

"Never too busy for you. What do you need?"

A short while later, Severin and Srulik are riding together in Srulik's old black Mercedes sedan. The driver's seat and front passenger seat both have beaded seat covers, and the radio is tuned, as always, to the army radio station. Srulik maintains that's the only good news source.

"Want a candy?" Srulik pops open the glove compartment to reveal a stash of lemon sucking candies.

Severin checks his phone. "No, thanks. My blood sugar is actually where it's supposed to be right now, so I'll just enjoy the rare moment."

"It's hard to be sick," says Srulik, clucking his tongue. "Oy, my sweet Yaelie. She's sick, too, and it makes me crazy that I can't do anything about it."

Severin nods and pushes his glasses up his nose. He knows all about Srulik's daughter Yael's cystic fibrosis, and how she, too, is waiting for an organ transplant. She needs new lungs, or she will die.

Srulik clears his throat. "But she's a fighter, my Yaelie. She's a real fighter. I know she'll get through this."

"She's a great girl."

"The best! She's the best thing that ever happened to Manya and me," Srulik gushes. "I tell you, I am the luckiest man in the world being her father. And my granddaughter, Tiki...well she's just the cherry on the ice cream cake."

Severin laughs. "You mean the icing on the cake. Or the cherry on the ice cream."

"Ich, no, I hate icing. I mean the cherry on the ice cream cake!"

It's a quick ride, about twenty minutes, and then Srulik turns his car through the Jaffa Gate into the Old City. Divided into four quarters: Jewish, Christian, Armenian, and Muslim, the Old City houses some of their holiest places. It is the site of the Western Wall, the Church of the Holy Sepulchre, and the Dome of the Rock. Severin feels safest in the Old City because he has been told there will never be a major attack there, because the neighborhood is sacred to so many. Only the uniformity of the cobblestone streets and buildings made out of Jerusalem stone (as is required by city law) belie the cultural and religious differences between the quarters.

The Old City was walled off in the sixteenth century by the Turkish Sultan, Suleiman the Magnificent; seven of its original eight gates are still in use. Cars are not allowed in much beyond the gates during the day, and the labyrinth of narrow alleyways and twisting roads makes it hard to navigate anything much bigger than a donkey cart. The lack of modern transportation combined with the heady aroma of spices and bread transports Severin to ancient times.

In fact, when he first came to the Old City two decades ago, he was overcome with emotion. "These are the same streets upon which Jesus walked," he marveled. He had kneeled down to touch the smooth cobblestones, and swore he felt the Holy Spirit upon him.

Twenty years later, Severin no longer marvels at the cobblestones. They're a nuisance. He's grateful the rainy season is over because the Old City streets are notoriously slippery when wet.

Srulik stops the car just beyond the Jaffa Gate, at the far end of the Christian Quarter.

"I'll see you soon, my friend."

"*Shabbat shalom*," says Severin.

He waves hello to the man selling oval-shaped sesame rolls from a giant wooden wheelbarrow on the sidewalk and walks carefully down the alleyway, past rows of dusty gray, attached houses four stories high, looking for cats as he walks. Like a true Franciscan, he loves all animals; like a true Jerusalemite, he is bothered by the mass of strays. Israel is home to one million feral cats—more than almost any country in the world—and at least one hundred thousand of them are in Jerusalem. Folklore says the cats were brought in by the British Mandate to get rid of a rat problem, and the relatively mild climate combined with the large availability of garbage helped the cat population flourish.

The government has tried different programs to get rid of them, to feed them, to spay or neuter them, all to no avail. Severin always carries a bag of dry kibble in his rucksack, and he leaves handfuls in various bowls that some of the Old City residents leave outside their doors. He's the Pied Piper of cats, as they appear from their hiding places and follow Severin in search of more food.

Back at the San Savior Monastery, the two cats that Severin domesticated greet him with loud meowing as soon as he opens the door to the rectory. Thomas and Aquinas—gray and orange-and-white-striped, respectively—stretch their bodies to the ground and wait for Severin to pet them.

"Hold on, lads." Severin hobbles to the wooden chair in the corner and plops down with a sigh of relief. He takes off his socks and sandals and looks at his swollen ankle. It's puffy and bruised, but definitely not broken. "Okay, not too bad. I'm okay."

The cats leap up onto his lap and, as he caresses them, purr contentedly. Severin always loved the feel of the cats' soft fur, how sliding his fingers through the fluff felt therapeutic and relaxing. But tonight, he can't help but compare petting the cats to holding baby Hadas. The fur suddenly feels strange. Before he met Hadas, he had never felt very comfortable with the human touch. He barely ever got more than a handshake from anyone throughout most of his life.

Severin may be helping Hadas, but he knows she is helping him, too. He can't explain why holding her is making up for him, having barely ever been held, but he has a feeling of closure that he never realized he needed.

"Father Severin, why do you look pained? Are you feeling unwell?" Michael strides hurriedly over to Severin, his robe swishing.

Severin shrugs. "I'm fine. I hurt my ankle this morning, and it's the first chance I've had all day to rest it. Nothing to worry about."

"I'm glad that's all it is. I was worried you were in one of your moods again."

"Contemplating my life is not a mood, Friar Michael. It's my job."

Michael's bright blue eyes widen, and the scar on his temple flushes red. He runs his fingers through his shiny black hair and stares at Severin.

"So, it's a testy mood, I see, not a contemplative one." Michael turns on his heel to leave. "When you've put your anger away, I'll be here to talk."

Severin nudges the cats off his lap and hangs his head. He shouldn't have snapped at Michael. The kid is hypersensitive, he thinks, but we all carry emotional baggage that shapes us. Ever since telling him that he's considering adopting Hadas, Michael has been strange with him.

Lord, forgive me, I should have been kinder, he thinks. Severin raises his head to apologize to Michael, but it's too late. He's already left the room.

***

L ATER THAT EVENING, SEVERIN is torn between returning to his room early to go to bed or waiting until much
later, when hopefully Michael will already be asleep. He avoided Michael all through dinner and evening prayers, and then
he closed himself in his office while he worked on his Sunday
sermon. He doesn't want to hurt Michael's feelings, but he also
doesn't want another confrontation.

One night about two months ago, after they had finished
their bedtime prayers, shut the light, and each had climbed into
his own bed, Severin swore Michael to secrecy, then revealed his
dream of adopting Hadas.

Michael sounded very confused. "I don't understand. Why
would you do that?"

"Because I love her!" Severin sputtered. "And because I don't
want her to spend her childhood in an orphanage like I did."

"But you can't have a child in a monastery."

"I know. I would have to leave."

"Leave? This is your life. You made a vow." Michael turned
to face the wall.

"I'm well aware of my vows, and I don't take this decision
lightly. I am unwavering in my faith."

"You should have faith that God will provide Hadas with a
real family."

"Why someone else? We're already bonded. Maybe God sent
me specifically for this reason?" said Severin. Then, in a singsong

voice: "*Perhaps I have attained this royal position for just such a crisis.*"

"Don't go quoting the Book of Esther to me, Severin," said Michael. "You're no biblical heroine."

Severin ignored the sting. "Michael, did you ever think that I might want a family of my own? I have no relatives. I want to belong to someone."

"You belong to me," whispered Michael.

Severin was speechless for a moment. "Michael, you and I will always be brothers, but I don't belong to you."

Severin waited a moment for Michael to respond, but Michael stayed facing the wall and remained quiet.

"Please, let's stop bickering. This is only a dream, and unless I get a transplant, I shouldn't even be dreaming. I can't raise a child on my own in my current condition. Please try to understand me."

Michael turned to face him. "I don't understand you. You're wishing for someone to die so that you can live out a dream?"

Severin winced. Of course, this was something he thought about often. He remembered witnessing an organ donor "honor walk" during one of his volunteer days at the hospital. Doctors, nurses, some patients, and friends of the organ donor—a young man in his twenties who had been in a motorcycle crash—lined the halls and clapped while he was wheeled into the operating room. For a moment, the sadness of the situation was almost forgotten in the cheering and whistling. But when he looked at the donor's family walking behind the hospital bed, with tears streaming down their cheeks and the mother audibly wailing, he was gutted.

"I'm not wishing for anyone to die, Michael. You know everything is God's will. I'm just praying that I can be healthy enough to raise a child."

"You'll have to pray for God's forgiveness. You swore to commit to a life of poverty, chastity, and obedience."

"Michael, please! I know very well what I've committed myself to. But aren't people allowed to change? Do I have to be the same person I was at eighteen?"

"One of the things I've always respected and admired about you, Father Severin, is your dedication to the Church. Everything you do is with Christ in mind. Perhaps you need to pray on this a bit more."

As Severin rehashes this scene in his mind, he resolves to talk with Michael again. Michael is right, after all. He *is* the closest thing Severin has to a real family. They'll talk in the morning, he promises himself. Always better to talk when the sun is up.

***

SEVERIN WAKES EARLY SUNDAY morning, before sunrise. He's grateful that Michael is still asleep. He checks his phone to see his blood sugar, and right away takes some insulin. His blood sugar is always high in the morning, but it's even higher than normal because he did so little exercise yesterday. He presses his foot down on the floor. It's better, but still tender. No long walks today, either.

The church opens in about two hours for prayer, with the first Mass in English and Latin at nine o'clock, and the Arabic Mass following afterward. Beforehand, Severin likes to work in the garden, as a way of privately communing with God and setting his intentions for the day.

He walks slowly through the vaulted passageway to the courtyard. Small pots of different herbs line the short wall alongside the walkway: rosemary, basil, sage, thyme, oregano. Severin rubs the rosemary needles as he passes by and sniffs the sweet-pungent smell on his fingers. The weather is warmer than usual for early April, and Severin feels hot even though the sun is not yet completely risen.

Severin's favorite part of the monastery is the garden. As a lonely little boy living in the convent in Ireland, he talked to the plants and the animals living outside. The nuns were pleased—a true Franciscan! they said—and they cultivated his talent for gardening. It was the only time they took a real interest in him. They provided him with tools and seeds, and he grew vegetables and herbs and many beautiful flowers.

Here in the monastery garden, Severin has divided the square area into four parts, building a trellis out of wood for the roses, and connecting it to the vaulted walkway leading to the clock tower. In one corner, he's planted fruit trees of all the biblical fruits that grow in Israel: lemons, etrogs, grapes, pomegranates, figs, and almonds. A nearly one-hundred-fifty-year-old olive tree sits in the center, its gnarled branches grooved deep so that it looks like someone traced it with a lead pencil. There had been a date palm off to the side that was very old, too, but the rare snowstorm that hit Jerusalem earlier that winter knocked it down.

Another trellis with bougainvillea covers the archway into the garden, and Severin decides to start there this morning, clipping and pruning the vines to encourage more blooms. He plucks off a flower that's browning at the edge of its bright pink center, and wipes it across his cheek. It's so soft, like baby Hadas. Severin's eyes well up. He adjusts his glasses, pushing them up on his nose.

"I thought I'd find you here," calls Michael from across the garden.

Severin waves hello. "Friar Michael, I'm glad you found me. I'm sorry we didn't get to talk last night."

Michael nods. "Me too. How's your ankle?"

"It's better, much better, thank you."

Michael runs his fingers through his hair. "I'm trying to understand this need for a family, but what about our purpose as monks? As the Custodians? You know better than I do that our numbers are dwindling here," says Michael. "We are fighting the holy fight! Do you want us to be pushed out of Jerusalem? We're letting the Jews and Arabs take over everything and we have to stop it. This land is ours, too!"

Severin smiles. "I'm glad you are so passionate, Michael. We've taught you well."

"Don't patronize me! What kind of a man of God are you if you're willing to give up fighting just to fulfill your own petty wishes?"

"I'm not sure I would call parenting petty, Friar Michael." Severin again pushes his glasses up on his nose. "I want to try to make you understand, but at the end of the day, only I will have to live with my decision. And as I've told you many times, right now this is a moot point because, as a sick person, I can never adopt Hadas."

"Sometimes I wonder if you want to adopt a baby just so you can justify getting a pancreas, so you can put a value on your life." Michael comes closer so that his nose is practically touching Severin's. "We are just servants of God, and what's God's wish will be ours."

Severin feels Michael's breath on his face and immediately steps back. "That's enough."

"There you go again, cutting the conversation short," Michael says. "We don't have a vow of silence in this monastery, Father Severin. Before you do something that you will surely regret, I suggest you talk it through with a true servant of God. If not me, then another of the friars."

Thomas and Aquinas wander into the garden just then, seemingly lured by the chirping of the birds in the concrete birdbath behind the date palm stump. Severin crouches down and pets them.

"I've got to go review my sermon. We can talk later, Friar Michael."

***

After Sunday Mass, Severin hears confessions and gives absolution to sinners. Every other day of the week Severin does some sort of community service, but on Sundays he dedicates the day to God. He stays in the monastery, administering whatever Church duties are necessary and running all of the prayer services. He's looking forward to performing a baptism later today for a baby of long-time parishioners who suffered through years of infertility.

It's nearly Easter, so before the baptism Severin is preparing a guide for Holy Week for his parishioners. He has to work on the website as well as update brochures for all of the visitors. He's in the office when Michael bursts in.

"Did you hear the news? There's been a bombing. A bus on the highway just outside of Jerusalem."

Severin's stomach lurches. He remembers tending to victims of the pizzeria bombing years earlier—the sickly stench of the blood, the moaning and the crying…he can't bear it.

"We need to go to the hospital to help the chaplains," urges Michael.

"I can't go," says Severin, shaking his head. "I have the Stevens' baptism in a few hours, and besides, my foot is in bad shape. I can barely walk."

"It's important that there's a Christian presence, Father Severin."

"Certainly, Friar Michael," replies Severin. "You go, and I'll stay here and finish up everything I was doing for Holy Week. And of course, I'll pray for the victims."

Michael turns on his heel and leaves without saying goodbye.

***

A T TWO IN THE afternoon on Sunday, the Stevens family arrives for baby Joseph's baptism. The Stevens family is small, just Marlene and John, their parents, and John's brother. Severin has performed hundreds of baptisms, but he has never paid as much attention to the baby as he does today. The sweet boy, Joseph, is only two months old—but compared to tiny baby Hadas he seems huge. He has pinchable cheeks, little folds of fat creasing into his wrists, and creamy skin the color of a peach.

Severin gives his usual short speech before the ceremony, talking to the parents about their roles in raising Joseph as a good Christian. But when the moment comes to dip his finger in the holy water and make a sign of the Holy Cross on baby Joseph's smooth forehead, Severin finds himself tingling. He looks closely at the baby, who smiles and gurgles at him, and he feels a peace come over him. Severin notices the usually dull metal chandelier that hangs over the altar is now shining with the rays of the afternoon sun streaming through the stained glass windows. Am I looking for a sign, or is this a sign, he wonders. He'll try to discuss it with Michael, and maybe that will help smooth the rift between them. Michael loves looking for the hand of God in everyday things.

A few hours later, though, Michael is still not back from the hospital. Severin is trying to stay awake, but he's exhausted. He fainted twice that afternoon, luckily both times in the presence of other monks. He goes to sleep with the promise in his head of making things better with Michael.

Finally, around eleven o'clock, Michael enters their bedroom. The light's still on, but Severin is sound asleep. Michael whispers his name, to no avail. He flips off the overhead light, and the room is shrouded in darkness. It's a moonless night, so only the faint glow of the outdoor lamp is visible through the window.

Just then, Severin's phone rings. An unfamiliar name flashes on the caller ID. Michael doesn't answer it. Severin doesn't seem to have heard anything.

The phone rings again. It's the same unfamiliar name. Michael stands by Severin's bed, and calls his name, but Severin doesn't move. The phone screen flashes with a text: "We have a pancreas! Call ASAP!"

Michael stays rigid, facing Severin lying in the bed. He puts the phone face down on the night table. Severin is still in a deep sleep, snoring lightly. Michael leaves the room.

Heart

"I SAW HER BOOBS when she leaned over," says Youssef Al Najjar. He leans back against his pillow, closes his eyes, and smiles. "It was a good day."

"Why do you always get all the luck?" asks Yosef Peretz from the bed across the room, without looking up from playing Candy Crush on his phone. It's a Sunday evening in early April, and visiting hours are over for the day. "No pretty girls ever come to visit me."

"I'm a babe magnet, what can I say?"

"Yeah, right. She was probably your cousin or something."

Youssef laughs. "She was, actually! But who cares? I still saw boobs."

Yosef laughs, too, first just a chuckle, but then he dissolves into a fit of hysterical giggles. The jerking of his chest sets off one of the alarms, and a nurse runs in to check the monitors.

"YoYos! Take it easy," she says. "Don't make me run in here a hundred times a day."

Youssef and Yosef are known as "The YoYos" on the pediatric cardiology floor of Hadassah Medical Center. They've been there for a while—Youssef nearly a month and Yosef almost three—while they wait for heart transplants. Their wide blue room is sectioned off in the middle with yellow curtains that can separate the area into two rooms, but now the boys like to be together, so they keep them open. One wall is windowed, with views of the green pine and cypress trees in the Jerusalem forest outside. The boys' beds are positioned opposite each other and the walls are painted with aquarium murals to try to camouflage the many medical devices and machines. A giant red coral reef is painted just above Yosef's head, and Youssef teases him that he looks like an underwater unicorn.

One is an Arab (Youssef) and the other is Jew (Yosef), but both are teenage boys from Jerusalem, and they are so close in age (sixteen and fifteen, respectively) and appearance they might be brothers. The regular hospital staff is able to differentiate between the YoYos, but when first meeting them, most people need to look at their charts to tell them apart. They both have dark hair, sparse facial fuzz, and naturally dark skin, although now they appear more ashen from their advanced cardiac diseases.

Yosef crumples a sheet to his mouth to stifle his laughter. It's ironic that as he and Youssef get weaker, their friendship gets stronger. Their friends' visits have become much less frequent, and even their families can't dedicate all day to sitting with them in the hospital. A lot of the time, it's just the YoYos.

"Those flowers your cousin brought are really strong," says Yosef. "I can smell them even through the sheet."

The purple hyacinths are in an empty water bottle on the table next to Youssef. "I like them," he says. "It reminds me that it's spring. I hate that we don't feel the weather in here."

When they feel up to it, the boys are wheeled to the hospital garden for a few minutes each day. For early April, the weather has been unseasonably warm, and the blooming flowers and budding trees are a stark contrast to the cold linoleum and antiseptic smell of the hospital.

Youssef picks up his phone and starts watching a YouTube video about basketball dunks. Yosef stares into space.

"How do you think he'll die?" asks Yosef.

"What? Who?" Youssef doesn't put down his phone.

"The person whose heart you'll get."

"Why do you always say it's me?" Youssef sounds exasperated. He looks up from his game. "You've been sicker longer than me. I bet you'll get one first."

"I may be too sick already," says Yosef sadly. "They're not going to waste a heart on me if they think it won't last."

"You're not too sick," Youssef says. "Your liver function was better than mine tonight."

"Well, whatever. How do you think the donor is going to die?"

"For sure a motorcycle accident. Don't they call them donor cycles?"

"It depends how he crashes. He might be too messed up."

"It matters how he falls, like if his skull is all bashed in, but his body is okay."

"Yeah." Yosef is quiet. "It's weird, isn't it, wishing that some-one will die?"

"Well, we're not killing the guy," says Youssef. "And in a way, a little part of the donor stays alive."

"Well, that creeps me out even more, I think. What if he was an asshole? Will I suddenly turn into one, too?"

"Suddenly?" laughs Youssef. "Come on, bro. It doesn't work that way."

"It might," insists Yosef. "I heard of someone who hated tomatoes and then got a new heart and now he loves tomatoes."

"What if we get a girl's heart and then we love boys, so we turn gay?"

Silence. Then both boys erupt with laughter.

"Nah, not gonna happen! Not with our boob obsessions!"

***

YOSEF HAS BEEN SICK for almost five years. He has a rare, inherited illness called arrhythmogenic right ventricular cardiomyopathy (ARVC), a progressive genetic condition that causes muscle cells in the ventricle wall to die. The muscle is replaced by fat and scar tissue, which causes irregular heart rhythms.

When he was thirteen years old, just after his bar mitzvah, Yosef fainted during a game of basketball. His parents, Anat and Shlomo, attributed it to the heat and ignored it. Then it happened twice more, both times while running for a layup.

Yosef complained that even when he wasn't exercising, he could feel his heart fluttering like a butterfly in his chest. After many medical tests, he was diagnosed with ARVC.

It would have been devastating for any family but was particularly hard for Yosef's. When he was a baby, his maternal grandparents were killed in a car accident, so Yosef's family had to move back to Israel from the United States to care for his great-grandmother. His younger and only sibling, Miriam, has Down syndrome. They live in Rechavia, a large, Jewish, residential neighborhood in the center of Jerusalem, without any of their extended family. Everyone else is in America, except one relative, an elderly cousin who lives in a nursing home a few hours' drive away.

"How could lightning strike us twice?" Yosef once overheard his mother ask a friend on the phone. "We've already been through a cardiac surgery with Miriam's congenital defect. I don't think I can bear it again."

Now, despite having a defibrillator surgically implanted two years ago, Yosef's heart is rapidly deteriorating, and he needs round-the-clock monitoring, as well as a continuous infusion of milrinone, a cardiac medication that helps the heart contract and relax. He has a PICC (peripherally inserted central catheter) line—a long, thin tube inserted into his upper left arm that carries the medicine through the veins into his heart. To keep it free of germs, there is a cap over the end of the PICC that sticks out of his arm and is taped down to his skin. He also wears EKG leads on his chest to monitor his heart, and a pulse oximeter on the pointer finger of his right hand.

Lately, Yosef finds it hard to breathe even while he is resting in bed. He's constantly exhausted, and his physical therapy had to be decreased from lifting light weights to simple stretches. When he walks down the hallway, either for exercise or to go to the game room, he leans on the handles of his wheelchair for support. Sometimes now, he even needs to stop midway to rest. He's miserable.

Youssef is miserable, too, but unlike Yosef, who has been sick for years, Youssef's illness came on rapidly. He's a year older, sixteen, and because he has only been sick for a short while, he still retains a semblance of his buff, muscular body. Youssef suffers from viral myocarditis, an inflammation of the heart muscle that is caused by a virus.

He had been a healthy, active teenager when sometime in the beginning of February, he became very fatigued. He usually played basketball with his friends for an hour or two every day after school, but he could barely get through a game without needing to sit and take a break. He coughed a lot and complained that his chest hurt. Youssef had gotten sick with the flu in January, so his mother Fatima thought he might just be taking a long time to recover.

One night, Fatima was in the kitchen of their small apartment in Abu Tor, a mixed Arab-Jewish neighborhood on a hillside in Jerusalem, south of the Old City, when she heard Youssef breathing very heavily from the living room. She rushed in to check on him. He tried to talk, but then began vomiting. His forehead was hot to the touch, while his hands were pale and cold. She called Omar, Youssef's father and her husband, and told him to rush home from work—something was terribly wrong with their son. At Hadassah Medical Center, doctors quickly diagnosed Youssef with myocarditis, and kept him overnight until he could be seen by the pediatric cardiologist. The prognosis wasn't very encouraging:

"With viral myocarditis, it's the rule of thirds: a third of the patients will recover completely, a third will need to stay on long-term heart medications, and a third will need a heart transplant."

"A heart transplant!" Fatima cried. "But that makes no sense...he's only been sick for a few weeks."

"Will I be able to play basketball?" Youssef asked.

"Not until you have a healthy heart," said the doctor.

"How long will that take?"

"I really don't know. It depends if you heal on your own, or if you'll need a transplant."

Youssef cried for the first time in years. Basketball was his life. He wasn't a great student, but he excelled on the court. Playing ball was the only thing that made him happy.

Within a matter of weeks, however, Youssef went from being a little tired to barely being able to walk. His heart was enlarged and failing fast. A month ago, doctors implanted a mechanical pump called the Heartmate 3 LVAD (a left ventricular assist device) into his chest, to help his weakened heart deliver blood throughout the rest of the body. The doctor explained that the LVAD was not a cure, rather just a bridge to a heart transplant. The LVAD wire pokes out of an incision in Youssef's upper abdomen and is attached to a controller that he wears as a belt. The controller is either connected to a battery pack, or to a power device plugged into the wall.

The doctor warned Fatima not to check Youssef's pulse, because he won't have one with the LVAD. It pumps the blood in a continuous flow, so there's no noticeable rhythm.

Technically Youssef could wait at home for the transplant, but the incision site keeps getting infected, so he's been hospitalized for weeks. He has a tube in his chest to drain the pus from the infection, as well as an IV inserted into the top of his hand, to deliver antibiotics to treat the infection. He also has EKG leads on his chest, which are attached to a heart monitor.

Both Yosef and Youssef are listed status 1A—the highest priority—for heart transplants.

***

WHEN YOUSSEF GOT THE LVAD implanted, he was put in a single room on the PCICU (Pediatric Cardiac Intensive Care Unit) while he recovered from the surgery. But once it was clear to the doctor that he would need a longer hospitalization because of the recurring infection, it was decided that he should share a room with another patient, so he would feel less lonely and have a support system.

"What the fuck is this?" he raged, when Fatima told him he would be moved into a double room. "Can't the one thing I get out of this be finally not having to share a room?"

"It'll be good for you," said Fatima. "You'll have someone to talk to who knows exactly what you're going through."

"I don't want to talk to anyone."

That Friday, when Youssef moved in, Anat and Miriam were visiting Yosef. Yosef's father runs a corner grocery market, so he was busy with people shopping for *Shabbat*. Anat was just about to leave when there was a knock at the door, and a nurse wheeled in Youssef. His mother followed behind.

Miriam had been sitting on the floor, playing with her doll. Her blonde hair was pulled into two pigtails on the sides of her head, and she wore tiny gold star earrings, and round, bright purple glasses. When Fatima walked into the room, Miriam scrambled over to her with arms extended, shouting: "Fati!"

Everyone else in the room looked confused.

"Miri! What a surprise to see you here!" said Fatima. "Is this your brother?"

Miri smiled widely. "Yosef."

Anat stood up and waved to Fatima from across the room. "Hi, I'm Anat Peretz. I guess you know Miriam."

"Yes, I'm her hydrotherapist at Shalva. My name is Fatima Al Najjar," said Fatima.

Shalva is an educational center in Jerusalem for people with disabilities that also provides therapies, recreation, and family support. It's located in the neighborhood of Bayit Ve'gan, right

by Shaare Zedek Medical Center. Miriam goes to school there
every day and has hydrotherapy sessions with Fatima three times
a week.

"Oh, yes!" said Anat. "Now that I'm looking at you closely,
I can sort of tell. But in the Facebook pictures, you're normally
wearing a bathing cap and goggles, so I didn't recognize you at
first."

Fatima tugged at her hijab. "Yes, I look different now."

"For how long have you been working at Shalva?"

"Five years."

There was an awkward silence, and the mothers both re-
treated to their respective son's bed. Fatima started to unpack
Youssef's bag into the drawers of the night table next to his bed.
Youssef mouthed to her: "Close the curtain!"

"I'm sorry Anat, Yosef, Miri. Would you mind if I closed the
privacy curtain for a little while? I think Youssef is going to rest."

"Of course! We'll get out of here soon so it can be quiet, don't
worry."

After everyone had gone, a Russian nurse named Olga came
in to check on the boys. She pulled the yellow curtains open so
the boys could see each other. "Youssef, meet Yosef. Yosef, meet
Youssef."

Youssef didn't look up from his phone.

"Hi," said Yosef.

"Talk to each other," said Olga. "I'll be back in a few minutes."

"What's wrong with your heart?" asked Yosef.

"It's fucking broken, idiot," said Youssef. "Why the hell else would I be here?"

"Is that an LVAD battery pack next to your bed?"

"Why are you asking me so many stupid questions?"

"We're in the same boat, that's all I was trying to say."

"We're not anything the same." Youssef glowered.

The boys didn't talk again the rest of the night.

The next morning, Youssef raged. He cursed at everyone that came into the room. He missed basketball, his friends, his almost-girlfriend.

"I shouldn't be here. I belong out on the court, sinking baskets. I need to get back to the gym. I was about to get a girlfriend." He seethed constantly and berated Yosef. "I'm not a weakling. Look at you, with your arms like sticks, just lying there in bed. You don't *do* anything, you just sit around. I'm not like that. I'm a mover and a shaker. I hustle."

Yosef was silent.

Nurse Olga chastised Youssef, telling him to calm down or it would raise his blood pressure. She closed the curtains between the beds.

Later that day, Anat came to visit Yosef, and he whispered to her that Youssef was giving him a hard time.

"Let's go for a walk, *motek*," she said. "I know it's hard, but you have to keep up your strength." She helped him wheel out his IV pole and the pole with the monitors, and together they walked down the hall, with Yosef pushing his wheelchair and Anat pushing the poles.

"*Ema*, I can't stand it! It's bad enough being in the hospital, but I can't be with someone so mean!" Yosef's eyes welled up with tears, and his lips quivered as he talked.

"I know, *motek*, I'll see what I can do."

"But you really don't know!" Yosef sat down in the wheelchair, his chest heaving. He struggled to talk. "It's so hard being here. I'm all alone, without you, without *Abba* or Miriam, without any of my friends. The nurses come in at all hours, poking and prodding and checking, and I never have any privacy or anything. It's awful and I hate it!"

"Oh, Yosef, I would do anything to fix this. Anything."

"I just want to go home."

Anat bit her lip and tears. She kissed Yosef on the top of his head as she pushed him to the game room. They sat there for a while in silence, and then Yosef said he needed to sleep.

The next day, Child Life sent a therapist named Rina to help Youssef channel his anger and use his competitive spirit through art therapy. For three consecutive days, she led Youssef and Yosef in speed painting contests, and yelled: "Brush it to crush it!" They vied with spin art machines, and she encouraged them: "Spin it to win it!" The cheering was so ridiculous that the boys ended up laughing, and it helped to break the tension between them. She dubbed them "The YoYos," and the nickname stuck.

The YoYos warmed quickly to Rina, and they also liked Olga, the nurse who worked the night shift. When the last of the boys' visitors left for the night, she would sit in their room for a few minutes, telling them what it was like growing up in Russia, waxing nostalgic about ice skating and drifting snowflakes, and asking them questions about their lives.

Olga was in her early thirties, tall, with strawberry-blond hair worn in a tight bun, and a large chest that was emphasized by the V-neck in her fitted scrub top. She wore a gold locket necklace that rested right in the fold of her cleavage. When she leaned over to check something, the locket would swing like a pendulum and had a hypnotic effect on the boys.

Every night, after she left their room and shut the lights, Youssef would say: "Thank you, *Allah*, for giving me one tiny joy in this awful place."

And every night, Yosef would answer, "Amen."

"She's not so pretty, but those boobs…" Youssef sighed.

"Perfect," said Yosef.

"You ever see ones for real?"

"You mean like naked?" Yosef squirmed in his bed.

"Yeah."

"Nah. Have you?"

"Almost." Youssef sighed. "This girl was really into me before I got sick. She would come watch my basketball games and cheer for me. But now she doesn't even text me anymore so…I guess it's over."

"That sucks, I'm sorry."

"At least we have Olga."

***

S IX DAYS AFTER YOUSSEF moved in with Yosef, Anat went to Shalva for her parent support group. They meet every Tuesday and Thursday afternoon, gathering in the building's lobby café. She's been going to the group for four years, and it has been a lifeline for Anat.

Just as she was walking down the stairs from the cafe to the main lobby, Fatima called to her from below.

"Anat! Hi! Anat!"

Fatima was standing in the lobby, waving to Anat.

"Oh, hi Fatima! Isn't it funny? We've never seen each other here before, and now suddenly here we are."

"Well, we probably saw each other before, but didn't realize it."

Anat nodded.

"Are you here to pick up Miri?" Fatima asked.

"Yes, but I have a few minutes before her class ends. I come here every Tuesday and Thursday afternoon for my parent support group."

"Do you enjoy it?"

Anat pursed her lips. "Well, enjoy...is a strong word. I get something out of it. I've made nice friends. And it's good for me to see the happiness and energy of this place."

The lobby of Shalva has large, painted butterflies hanging in the high-ceilinged lobby, and the decor throughout the building is brightly colored and cheerful. Groups of singing children pass through, and the teenaged volunteers chatter excitedly as they walk.

"Yes, it is a happy place," agreed Fatima. "Certainly a lot better than the hospital."

"Oh God, yes," said Anat. "I can't wait for Yosef to get out of there." She paused and took a deep breath. "I pray he'll get out of there alive."

Fatima put her hand on Anat's shoulder. "*Inshallah.*"

Anat smiled slightly, with her lips closed. "How are you doing? It must have been scary for Youssef to get sick so quickly."

"Terrifying. I still can't believe it. He was such a strong, active boy, and now...well, he seems like a different person."

"Illness changes your personality," said Anat. "Certainly, it's changed Yosef's. He was never the loudest kid, but now he's so quiet. He spends a lot of time playing video games and reading. I'm not sure how many of his friends are still texting him."

Fatima smoothed her hands on her pants and adjusted her hijab. "Would you mind if we talked outside? I love watching the kids on the playground, and the weather is so warm for this early in April."

Anat and Fatima walked out to the front of the building, to the large, inclusive playground with adaptive, wheelchair-accessible equipment. Able-bodied children as well as children with disabilities could play here together, so it was a favorite spot for the Shalva children and their siblings. The women sat on a bench underneath a palm tree.

"I'm glad the boys are getting along better," said Fatima. "I know Youssef has a temper. I'm sorry he took out his anger on Yosef."

"It's okay," said Anat. "I think Yosef understood not to take it personally."

"Yosef is probably the only one who can understand Youssef now. It's so hard to imagine what his life is like, and I'm his mother! I think his friends are just too far removed from the situation. And most of the time, he just played basketball with his friends, anyway, and he certainly can't do that now."

"Yosef loves basketball, too," said Anat. "And he was pretty good at it! But he had to give it up almost two years ago when his heart started to get worse. He just didn't have the energy."

Fatima sighed. They sat watching the children jump all around the playground, shrieking and laughing.

"It's weird to see the world going on like everything's normal," she said.

"That's the only thing better about the hospital," said Anat. "We're in an alternate reality there, but so is everyone. I don't feel so alone."

"I can't sleep anymore, can you?"

"Sleep? Ha! Only with a lot of whiskey..."

"I lie awake counting my fears," said Fatima. "I'm scared he'll die—of course, that's the thing that terrifies me the most. But also everything else: Is he in pain? Will he get a blood clot or have a stroke? Will the transplant go smoothly? Will he reject the heart? What if he gets too depressed just lying there in the hospital and...?" She gulped and squeezed her eyes shut.

"And what?"

"Well, I read that some kids get so depressed lying in the hospital that they cut their own LVAD wires." A single tear dripped down Fatima's cheek. "I'm worried that Youssef is already thinking about this. Like, maybe his wound keeps getting infected because he's purposely not being careful with the controller, and it keeps falling and slowly pulling out the driveline."

Anat took Fatima's hands in hers. "We can't despair, or we won't be able to stay strong for our boys. All we have is hope. That's all the doctors can give us, really. None of these medications or treatments will cure our boys. They're just buying them time."

Anat scribbled her number on a piece of paper and handed it to Fatima. "I'm here for you. Call me anytime."

***

As a Child Life therapist, one of Rina's jobs is to help the boys to understand any medical procedure they might need. One day, she came in with two iPads loaded with explanatory videos and brought sample surgical tools and other medical instruments so they could see what would be used. "How would you guys like to watch a heart transplant?"

"What?" Youssef looked alarmed.

"Right now?" Yosef struggled to speak.

"Not for real, guys, on the iPad. We don't do this with little kids, but I thought you guys were old enough that you might want to see what the surgery is about."

Rina is only about ten years older than the boys, and with her toothy smiles and perky personality, she easily assumed the role of big sister. She gave each boy an iPad, and walked from one side of the room to the other to point things out.

"The scariest part of the procedure to watch is probably opening up the chest, and I think we should skip that part," she said. "It's the least complicated, medically, but it's not fun."

"Yeah, they have to crack open your rib cage!" Yosef shuddered. "That must kill!"

"Well, it won't be painful while they're doing it, because you'll be totally asleep from the anesthesia," said Rina. "But after the surgery it can hurt. You'll have to be careful not to sneeze or cough, or even laugh too hard."

"If I'm still hanging with this guy, that won't be a problem, because his jokes are stupid," said Youssef, pointing his finger at Yosef.

"Haha. Aren't you hysterical?" said Yosef.

"Okay, guys. Do you see what happens next? The patient will have already been hooked up to a heart-lung bypass machine, to help oxygenated blood flow through the body during surgery."

The boys both looked intently at their screens.

"And then, after the chest is open, the surgeon will remove the diseased heart and sew the donor heart into place. Then they'll attach all the blood vessels to the new heart, and blood flow should resume almost immediately."

"And that's it?" Yosef asked.

"That's the main part of the surgery," said Rina. "We can do the post-op stuff now, too, or we can take a break and I can show you that video another day."

"I'm tired," said Youssef, yawning. "Let's do it another day."

***

As the boys became friendlier, so too did their families. Youssef has three siblings and many cousins and always has a rotating cast of visitors. Yosef has a much smaller family, and so over the past month, the families have blended their visits. The curtains stay open all the time, because visitors come for the YoYos, not just for one of the boys. Fatima brings her famous *knafeh*, a dessert made with tiny, buttered noodles that are covered with crumbles of goat cheese and then seared on both sides until golden. She used to pretend that she made it herself, but now that the families know each other better she confessed that she buys it from a special sweets store in Nablus.

The fathers aren't there very often, because of their work schedules. Shlomo, Yosef's father, has a worker helping him at the grocery, but he doesn't trust him enough to leave the store for long. Omar, Youssef's father, works as the catering manager in the Inbal hotel, a luxury hotel in the center of Jerusalem. Two weeks before Passover, the kitchens are even more chaotic than usual, because as a kosher hotel, they have to be scrupulous not to have any bread products come in contact with the food being prepared for Passover. The hospital has made exceptions for them to come very early in the morning or very late at night, but the fathers are only able to come sporadically.

Only once since the boys have been sharing a hospital room have both fathers been there at the same time. It occurred the previous night, when both men arrived around five o'clock. They rode the elevator together, not realizing who the other was, until they both came to the door of the YoYos' room.

"Ah, you must be Youssef's father," said Shlomo. "I'm Shlomo Peretz. Nice to meet you."

"Omar Al Najjar. Pleasure."

The men shook hands and greeted the boys. After they bantered around with their sons, they turned on the television to Sport5 so the boys could watch an American NBA basketball game.

"So, I hear you work at the Inbal?"

"Yes, I've been there for almost ten years. Gearing up for Passover...the hardest holiday."

"It's a pain, yes," said Shlomo. "We aren't very religious, but we do keep the laws of not eating any bread on Passover."

"Do you have a Seder?"

"Yes, of course. We're very traditional, just maybe not so strict with everything."

"Well, we are one-hundred-and-ten percent strict at the Inbal," said Omar.

"I bet you know more about the rules than we do!"

Omar chuckled. "If you want, come by the hotel on one of the days of the holiday, and I'll be glad to have you for a meal as my guests."

"Well, that's very kind of you, thank you." Shlomo tapped Yosef on the shoulder. "Hey, you hear Omar invited us to the Inbal for a meal on *Pesach?*"

Yosef gave Shlomo a death stare. "*Abba*, how dumb are you? *Pesach* is in two weeks. There's no chance I'll be out by then, even if by some miracle I get a heart tomorrow."

Shlomo smacked his forehead. "Oy! I'm such an idiot. I'm sorry, *motek*, I wasn't thinking."

"Hey bro, don't worry, you're not missing anything," said Youssef. "I had their Passover food once, and it was terrible!"

"You go there a lot?"

"Yeah, I play ball in the park right behind—Gan HaPa'amon (Liberty Bell Park)."

"No way!" Yosef said. "I used to play there all the time."

Gan HaPa'amon is a large park with a replica of the Liberty Bell, which is how it got its name. It's located in the Talbiyeh neighborhood of Jerusalem, right behind the Inbal hotel. The courts are located in the middle of the park, with built-in bleachers alongside the far court. Some of the local schools run leagues there, but as a public park, the courts are open to anyone.

The fathers stayed until visiting hours were over. After they left, the boys wondered if they had ever played basketball against each other.

"Were you one of those annoying Jewish kids who complained that we took your court?" Youssef asked. "I bet you were."

"I don't know," said Yosef. "But you guys are really rude, usually. I haven't played in a few years, though, since I got sicker."

"We would smoke you on the court."

"Maybe, I don't know. I don't think we ever played against you guys."

"Yeah, we don't usually play the Jews."

"Hey," Yosef clears his throat. "Did you care—I mean, did it matter to you when you realized you had to share a room with me and I'm Jewish?"

Youssef shrugged his shoulders. "Nah. I didn't care who you were. I didn't want to be with anyone. I didn't want to be in the hospital. I still don't."

"Yeah."

"What about you? Did you care that I'm Arab?"

"Well," Yosef hesitated. "I guess I felt a little intimidated by you. I don't really have any Arab friends. My only interactions have been on the court, and the Arab kids end up trash-talking us and fighting over who gets to play."

"But you're okay now?"

"Yeah, bro." Yosef reddened. "Don't make a big deal out of nothing."

"Hey—what's your top score in a game?"

"Forty-eight points."

"Yeah, right. How many three-pointers in a row?"

"Five."

"What a liar!"

***

ONE DAY, RINA BROUGHT paint-by-number kits to keep the YoYos occupied for an hour. Both boys were both getting weaker, and it was easier for her to bring projects to them than have them come to the crafts workshop room in the basement. They each sat in their bedside armchairs, with their tray tables in front of them. Youssef had a picture of a sailboat, and Yosef had a picture of a lighthouse.

"This is kind of boring, but I'll admit, it is relaxing," said Yosef, after the boys had been painting for a little while.

"Yeah, it's nice to focus on something mindless like this," echoed Youssef.

Rina clapped her hands. "Yay me! I thought you guys would like this."

She propped herself up on the wide ledge of the window and crossed her ankles. "Should I put on some music? I just made a new animal-themed playlist."

"Animal themed?" Yosef asked.

"Yeah, *Eye of the Tiger, Hungry Like the Wolf, Free Bird...*"

"Um, that's probably more appropriate for a trip to the zoo, but sure."

As the thumping beat of the first song started, Youssef asked: "Hey Rina, can I ask you something?"

"Sure."

"Do you know which one of us is listed higher for transplant?"

Yosef stared at Youssef, but Youssef kept his eyes focused on his canvas.

Rina hopped off the ledge and pulled out the elastic from her ponytail. She wound her hair into a bun and re-fastened the elastic.

"I think you both have the same status—1A—which means you both are in the highest category to get transplants if a donor heart becomes available."

"Yeah, but which one of us is higher?" Youssef held his paintbrush still.

"I really don't know," Rina said. "There are so many things that have to align: you and the donor have to have compatible blood types..."

"We're both Type A."

"Well, they do HLA marker testing—so even though you're both the same blood type one of you could still be a better match. Do you know what HLA markers are?"

The YoYos shook their heads.

Rina turned off the music. She scrolled through her iPad and found an image of a circle with lots of different-shaped icons sticking out of it, similar to a child's picture of a sun with rays. "HLA stands for human leukocyte antigens, which are proteins found on most of the cells in the body. The closer you match with the donor, the less likely you'll reject the heart."

"Well, how do we know what our HLA markers are?" asked Youssef.

"You don't need to know them, but about once a week when they take your blood, they test them to make sure they have the most up-to-date information. One type isn't better than another, it's just how closely you might match with the donor. Get it now?"

The boys nodded.

"The donor has to be of similar body size or smaller, to make sure the heart will fit in your rib cage."

"Youssef is a bit bigger than me," said Yosef. He dabbed his paintbrush into the red paint pot on his tray and focused intently on his canvas. Now Youssef was staring at him.

"Not by much," said Youssef. "I'm losing weight and muscle every day that I'm in this fucking place."

"Okay, Youssef." Rina turned off the music. "And you need to be in the same geographic location as the donor, but obviously..."

"Does the donor know who we are?" asked Yosef.

"No," said Rina. "And you won't know who the donor is, either, unless the family wants you to."

"I definitely wouldn't want to meet them," said Youssef.

"Why?"

"What if they were disappointed that it was me?"

"I'm sure they'd be thrilled to know they saved the life of a teenage boy."

"Yeah, but what if they were Jewish, and didn't like that I was Arab?"

Rina stood up and walked over to Youssef. "I can't speak for all Jewish people, but I think I can speak for a lot of us: no one would care. You're a human being."

"You just say that because you work in a hospital. Things are different here."

"Yo—would you be okay with a Jewish heart?" Yosef piped up. "Be honest."

Youssef put down his paintbrush and looked back and forth at Rina and Yosef. "Okay, honestly...a year ago I might have said no. But now I don't care who it's from, I just want to get the hell out of here and be normal again."

"I guess that's why people seem to get along in the hospital," said Rina. "Because you realize we're all the same inside."

She turned the music back on and admired the boys' paintings.

"So back to my original question," said Youssef. "Which one of us is higher?"

"I told you, I don't know," said Rina. "Things can change day-to-day, as well. They don't want to give a heart to someone so sick that the body is too weak to accept it, but they also need to give it to the sickest patient. It's a very delicate balance."

"Well, Yosef seems sicker than me, so I guess he'll get it."

"I don't think you guys should play that game," said Rina. "Hopefully, you'll both get hearts really soon. In the meantime, the one good thing I can tell you is that you're both old enough and big enough to accept an adult heart, which means that you both trump any adult waiting for a heart. Kids get to cut the line."

The YoYos continued painting in silence for a few minutes, absorbing the information. Rina's phone alarm dinged, and she told the boys they could keep working, but she would have to go to her next patient appointment.

After she left, Youssef stopped painting. "I've heard that sometimes a donor heart comes in but then they can't use it. Like, it's either too big or there's some problem with it, the arteries or something."

"Well, that would suck."

"Yeah." Youssef swallowed hard. "And then what if that's it? Like, there's no other heart and we just keep getting sicker?"

"Don't you think that's a good possibility? I mean, do you see how the doctors never look our parents in the eye?"

"And then what?"

"I guess we'll die."

"You seem pretty calm about that."

Yosef put down his paintbrush and looked at Youssef. "I've been sick for a lot longer than you. I've had time to think about this."

Youssef started to cry.

"Hey, bro, it's gonna be okay." Yosef pushed aside his tray and stood up. He grabbed his IV pole in one hand, and the pole with all the monitors in the other, and he slowly crossed the room to Youssef's side. He bent over Youssef's chair and gave him an awkward hug.

Youssef shook him off but pulled his hand in for a bro hand-shake. "Thanks, man."

Yosef wheeled his poles back to his side. "I find dark humor to be helpful. Like, for example, I've been planning my last meal for a while."

Youssef wiped the tears off his cheeks. "*Yalla.*"

"Okay, first, super spicy olives, fresh pita from Haba Pita, and hummus from Taim."

"No way, man," said Youssef. "The best hummus is Abu Shukri."

"I've never heard of that," said Yosef.

"Whaaaaat? Seriously?"

"Where is it?"

"The Old City."

"Well, it must be in the Muslim Quarter, if I've never been there."

Youssef nodded. "Yup. Well, when we get out of here, I'll take you there."

"Would you really go with me?"

"*Betach.* You're my bro."

***

L ATER THIS SUNDAY EVENING, after their laughter dies
down, and the YoYos see Olga's hypnotic pendant nestled
in her breasts, they talk while they play more video games. The
boys are supposed to be skyping into their classes and doing
schoolwork, but neither has the attention span or strength, and
no one is fighting them on it.

"And we start it all again tomorrow morning," says Youssef,
sighing.

"What?"

"Waking up and wondering if today is going to be the day. Or
are we just going to have another sucky day in this awful place,
lying here and getting sicker?"

Yosef can barely talk. His breath is ragged from all the laughing. He rasps. "So, tell me your dream day."

"What dream day?"

"Let's say you were healthy, but you didn't have to go to
school."

"Dude, at this point I *want* to go to school," says Youssef.

"I know, but I mean, if you had a day off, and you could do
anything you wanted, what would it be?"

"Am I rich?"

"Sure. You're rich and healthy and you've got nothing but
time on your hands."

Youssef whistles. "I'm a lucky guy!" He thinks for a minute,
and then says, "Honestly, a day at the beach with my cousins,
some great *shawarma* in a *laffa* for dinner, and then a nighttime
basketball game with my boys."

"That's it?"

"Yeah," says Youssef. "I'm a simple dude. Why, what about you?"

"I want to go to New York," says Yosef. "I was born there, but I haven't been back since I was a baby. I want to be in Times Square and see all the excitement. Eat hamburgers and fries. Go to an amusement park. And obviously, I want to fly first class to America and get driven to the airport in a Lambo."

"Sick."

Yosef takes shallow breaths. One of his monitors beeps, and the night nurse comes in to check that everything is okay. She gives him some oxygen through a cannula in his nose. "Just for a little bit," she says. "Until you're feeling better."

The nurse shuts the main light, and only the glow of the boys' phones illuminates the room.

"I don't think I'm going to make it," says Yosef.

"Yeah, except you're number one," says Youssef.

"What?"

"Number one. Don't you ever hear the nurse calling us One and Two?"

"I thought she was just talking about us as the two teenage boys."

"No, you dope," says Youssef. "We're one and two on the transplant list. You're sicker than I am—you're number one. If you've already been waiting for three months, what are the chances I am going to get a heart in time? I'm getting weaker every day."

"Well, then maybe you'll be number one."

"Maybe there will be a crazy car accident or something and there will be two hearts and we'll both get them."

"Maybe. Doubtful, but maybe."

***

THE USUAL SLEEPINESS OF the night shift changes dramatically an hour later, once it is certain there is a donor heart available. There's a flurry of activity as family members are called, and nurses and doctors hurry in and out of the room. One of the nurses tries to pull the curtains to section off the room, but the YoYos want to be able to see each other.

"I knew it would be you."

"I really thought it would be you."

The tension is palpable, as the contradictory emotions battle: fear and excitement and sadness and elation. Yosef and Youssef stare at each other with tearful eyes, just before it is time for the lucky boy to go to the operating room for the transplant surgery.

"See you on the basketball court."

"Don't pretend not to know me!"

*I*N ONE DAY, *I saved six lives.*

I had always hoped to make a change in the world. Back in January, my mom predicted I would. Neither of us ever dreamed it would happen this way.

At my funeral, thousands of mourners heard the rabbi finish his speech with the traditional Jewish refrain: "May her memory be a blessing." For the six people you just met, those were much more than empty words.

So, while my family might be feeling very unlucky right now, I hope that with time our house will once again be lively and happy, and I will know I have made them proud.

Author's Note

This is a work of fiction, inspired by the true story of my childhood friend, Alisa Flatow. In April 1995, when we were twenty years old, Alisa was on her way to a seaside hotel in Israel when a suicide bomber rammed his car into her bus and exploded himself. A piece of shrapnel struck Alisa fatally in her brain stem.

We had both been studying abroad that spring semester. Alisa was in Jerusalem, and I was in London. In those pre-Internet days, news traveled slowly, and foreign calls were two dollars a minute. But on that fateful Sunday, within an hour of learning about the bombing, my phone was ringing off the hook. Alisa was on the bus, in critical condition with a head injury.

We didn't have a prom queen at our high school or a popularity contest, but Alisa probably would have won both. She was a fun and cheerful person, with big, bright eyes and huge dimples. Everyone liked her. It was unfathomable that she was the first in our class to die.

For years, I struggled to make sense of her death, but as I got older, I realized that existential questions have no answers. Instead, I focused on the groundbreaking effect she had as a

Jewish organ donor in Israel. Historically, the concept of brain death under Jewish law and tradition was too murky to give a clear answer about whether organ donation was acceptable, and Israel suffered from a donor shortage. Alisa changed that. She was the catalyst for thousands of Jewish people in Israel and around the world signing on as organ donors.

I flew to Israel the day after Alisa's death, in time for the send-off at Ben Gurion Airport as her body was loaded into the cargo hold of a plane that would take her back to her native New Jersey. But it was the news conference the next day that has had the most lasting impact on me: Then-Prime Minister Yitzchak Rabin praising Alisa's family's heroic act, and proclaiming, "Alisa's heart is alive and beating here in Jerusalem."

Acknowledgments

I've felt like a liar for years, telling people I'm a writer when all I had was a stack of drafts. But my family believed in me, and it's because of their support that this book has finally been published.

Thank you first and foremost to my husband, Daniel. How fortunate I am that you've been in my life since I was a teenager. I've never had to explain why this story has been burning in me for so long, because you were there, too. We share values and dreams, and a deep love for each other and our children. You support me in every way, and I can never fully express my gratitude.

To my children—Gabriella, Zach, and Eliana—the three best people in the world, and I'm not just saying that because I'm your mother. I appreciate how you each encourage me and love me in your own unique ways. You make me happy and give purpose to my life.

I owe everything I am to my parents, Andrew and Beverly Geller. Mom and Dad, you instilled in me an intellectual curiosity and love for reading, among many other things, and you taught me to stand up for what I believe in. You're always there for me, and you love me unconditionally.

Thank you to my extended family for being wonderful people: my parents-in-law Paul and Louisa Wolf; my son-in-law, Evan Glick; my siblings, Aviva and Jonathan Laib; Josh and Adina Geller; Simon and Stefanie Wolf; Mikey and Yael Wolf; and all of my nieces, nephews, and cousins.

To the original Hoda, thank you for our barbershop talks, where you reinforced my belief that all human beings are the same and we should just try harder to get along.

And to the real Srulik—my grandmother Fela Kolat's first cousin, Holocaust survivor, pioneer of Israel, friend to all—you are the bedrock of our family. Your hard work will ensure our future.

I'm grateful to all of my writer friends, including: Marcia Bradley, Shelby Coppola, Julie Neches, Jackie Goldstein, Elizabeth Bonan, Ines Rodrigues, Eileen Palma, Susan Davidoff, and Ellen Hopkins. Thank you also to Sharon Levine, Jordana Schoor, Adina Galbut, Stacy Kent, and Lauren Wein, for your advice and support.

Thank you to Sarah Bedingfield for believing in my book. Without your expertise and encouragement, I would never have come this far.

Mike Kelly and Tim Hays—thank you for sharing your journalistic and publishing wisdom even though you barely know me, just because you care about Alisa's legacy.

Thank you to Peter Alson for ushering this book into the world.

I wish there had never been an inspiration to write this story. But in the nearly thirty years since Alisa was killed, there have been countless other victims of war and terror whose organs have been selflessly donated by their families. Every time I read about one of these donors, I immediately think of Alisa. She started it all.

Thank you, Alisa, for greeting me cheerily every morning at our lockers with a big smile. You were so much fun to be around. I'll always remember sharing a giant watermelon with you on our summer tour in Israel, slurping up the juice with giant straws and not caring that it dripped on our shirts. And unfortunately, I'll always remember the fateful day when you were killed. I know exactly what song I was listening to, what paper I was working on, what I was drinking. I'm so sorry that your life got cut short. You made an incredible impact on the world in your death; you would have made an even bigger one in your life. I'll never forget you.